There was a possibility they might repair their starship and go on again to their original destination.

Until the Ghost Wind blew . . .

There was a possibility that they might construct a safe Earthlike society right there on the alien planet where they had crashed.

Until the Ghost Wind blew . . .

There was a possibility that they might be the cleverest intelligent species on that world and could make themselves its lords and masters.

Until the Ghost Wind blew . . .

But until the coming of that strange air current, they would never be welcome to Darkover.

That was Darkover's way.

Darkover Landfall

by
Marion Zimmer Bradley

DAW BOOKS, INC.

DONALD A. WOLLHEIM, PUBLISHER

1301 Avenue of the Americas
New York, N. Y.   10019

Cover art by Jack Gaughan.

ACKNOWLEDGMENTS: The songs quoted in the text from the New Hebrides Commune are all from the *Songs of the Hebrides,* collected by Marjorie Kennedy-Fraser and published 1909, 1922, by Boosey and Hawkes. *The Seagull of the Land-Under-Waves,* English words by Mrs. Kennedy-Fraser, from the Gaelic of Kenneth MacLeod. *Caristiona,* words traditional, English by Kenneth MacLeod. *The Fairy's Love Song,* English words by James Hogg (adapted). *The Mull-Fisher's Song,* English words by Marjorie Kennedy-Fraser. *The Coolins of Rum,* English words by Elfrida Rivers, by special permission.

DEDICATION

To Lester Del Rey
with love, respect and admiration

FIRST PRINTING, DECEMBER 1972

PRINTED IN U.S.A.

Chapter
ONE

The landing gear was almost the least of their worries; but it made a serious problem in getting in and out. The great starship lay tilted at a forty-five degree angle with the exit ladders and chutes coming nowhere near the ground, and the doors going nowhere. All the damage hadn't been assessed yet—not nearly—but they estimated that roughly half the crew's quarters and three-fourths of the passenger sections were uninhabitable.

Already half a dozen small rough shelters, as well as the tentlike field hospital, had been hastily thrown up in the great clearing. They'd been made, mostly out of plastic sheeting and logs from the resinous local trees, which had been cut with buzz-saws and timbering equipment from the supply materials for the colonists. All this had taken place over Captain Leicester's serious protests; he had yielded only to a technicality. His orders were absolute when the ship was in space; on a planet the Colony Expedition Force was in charge.

The fact that it wasn't the *right* planet was a technicality that no one had felt able to tackle . . . yet.

It was, reflected Rafael MacAran as he stood on the low peak above the crashed spaceship, a beautiful planet. That is, what they could see of it, which wasn't all that much. The gravity was a little less than Earth's, and the oxygen content a little higher, which itself meant a certain feeling of well-being and euphoria for anyone born and brought up on Earth. No one reared on Earth in the twenty-first century, like Rafael MacAran, had ever smelled such sweet and resinous air, or seen faraway hills through such a clean bright morning.

The hills and the distant mountains rose around them in an apparently endless panorama, fold beyond fold,

5

gradually losing color with distance, turning first dim green, then dimmer blue, and finally to dimmest violet and purple. The great sun was deep red, the color of spilt blood; and that morning they had seen the four moons, like great multicolored jewels, hanging off the horns of the distant mountains.

MacAran set his pack down, pulled out the transit and began to set up its tripod legs. He bent to adjust the instrument, wiping sweat from his forehead. God, how hot it seemed after the brutal ice-cold of last night and the sudden snow that had swept from the mountain-range so swiftly they had barely had time to take shelter! And now the snow lay in melting runnels as he pulled off his nylon parka and mopped his brow.

He straightened up, looking around for convenient horizons. He already knew, thanks to the new-model altimeter which could compensate for different gravity strengths, that they were about a thousand feet above sea level—or what would be sea level if there were any seas on this planet which they couldn't yet be sure of. In the stress and dangers of the crash-landing no one except the Third Officer had gotten a clear look at the planet from space, and she had died twenty minutes after impact while they were still digging bodies out of the wreckage of the bridge.

They knew that there were three planets in this system: one an oversized, frozen-methane giant, the other a small barren rock, more moon than planet except for its solitary orbit, and this one. They knew that this one was what Earth Expeditionary Forces called a Class M planet—roughly Earth-type and probably habitable. And now they knew they were on it. That was just about all they knew about it, except what they had discovered in the last seventy-two hours. The red sun, the four moons, the extremes of temperature, the mountains all had been discovered in the frantic intervals of digging out and identifying the dead, setting up a hasty field hospital and drafting every able-bodied person to care for the injured, bury the dead, and set up hasty shelters while the ship was still inhabitable.

Rafael MacAran started pulling his surveying instruments from his pack but he didn't attend to them. He had needed this brief interval alone more than he had realized; a little time to recover from the repeated and terrible shocks of the last few hours—the crash, and a concussion which would have put him into a hospital on crowded, medically-hypersensitive Earth. Here the medical officer, harried from worse injuries, tested his reflexes briefly, handed him some headache pills, and went on to the seriously hurt and the dying. His head still felt like an oversized toothache although the visual blurring had cleared up after the first night's sleep. The next day he had been drafted, with all the other able-bodied men not on the medical staff or the engineering crews in the ship, to dig mass graves for the dead. And then there had been the mind-shaking shock of finding Jenny among them.

Jenny. He had envisioned her safe and well, too busy at her own job to hunt him up and reassure him. Then among the mangled dead, the unmistakable silver-bright hair of his only sister. There hadn't even been time for tears. There were too many dead. He did the only thing he could do. He reported to Camilla Del Rey, deputizing for Captain Leicester on the identity detail, that the name of Jenny MacAran should be transferred from the lists of unlocated survivors to the list of definitely identified dead.

Camilla's only comment had been a terse, quiet "Thank you, MacAran." There was no time for sympathy, no time for mourning or even humane expressions of kindness. And yet Jenny had been Camilla's close friend, she'd really loved that damned Del Rey girl like a sister—just why, Rafael had never known, but Jenny had, and there must have been some reason. He realized somewhere below the surface, that he had hoped Camilla would shed for Jenny the tears he could not manage to weep. Someone ought to cry for Jenny, and he couldn't. Not yet.

He turned his eyes on his instruments again. If they had known their definite latitude on the planet it would have been easier, but the height of the sun above the horizon would give them some rough idea.

Below him in a great bowl of land at least five miles across filled with low brushwood and scrubby trees, the crashed spaceship lay. Rafael, looking at it from this distance, felt a strange sinking feeling. Captain Leicester was supposed to be working with the crew to assess the damage and estimate the time needed to make repairs. Rafael knew nothing about the workings of starships—his

7

own field was geology. But it didn't look to him as if that ship was ever going anywhere again.

Then he turned off the thought. That was for the engineering crews to say. They knew, and he didn't. He'd seen some near-miracles done by engineering these days. At worst this would be an uncomfortable interval of a few days or a couple of weeks, then they'd be on their way again, and a new habitable planet would be charted on the Expeditionary Forces starmaps for colonization. This one, despite the brutal cold at night, looked extremely habitable. Maybe they'd even get to share some of the finder's fees, which would go to improve the Coronis Colony where they'd be by then.

And they'd all have something to talk about when they were Old Settlers in the Coronis Colony, fifty or sixty years from now.

But if the ship never did get off the ground again. . . .

Impossible. This wasn't a charted planet, okayed for colonizing, and already opened up. The Coronis Colony— Phi Coronis Delta—was already the site of a flourishing mining settlement. There was a functioning spaceport and a crew of engineers and technicians had been working there for ten years preparing the planet for settlement and studying its ecology. You couldn't set down, raw and unhelped by technology, on a completely unknown world. It couldn't be done.

Anyway, that was somebody else's job and he'd better do his own now. He made all the observations he could, noted them in his pocket notebook, and packed up the tripod starting down the hill again. He moved easily across the rock-strewn slope through the tough underbrush and trees carrying his pack effortlessly in the light gravity. It was cleaner and easier than a hike on Earth, and he cast a longing eye at the distant mountains. Maybe if their stay stretched out more than a few days, he could be spared to take a brief climb into them. Rock samples and some geological notations should be worth something to Earth Expeditionary and it would be a lot better than a climbing trip on Earth, where every National Park from Yellowstone to Himalaya was choked with jet-brought tourists three hundred days of the year.

He supposed it was only fair to give everyone a chance at the mountains, and certainly the slidewalks and lifts installed to the top of Mount Rainier and Everest and

8

Mount Whitney had made it easier for old women and children to get up there and have a chance to see the scenery. But still, MacAran thought longingly, to climb an actual wild mountain—one with no slidewalks and not even a single chairlift! He'd climbed on Earth, but you felt silly struggling up a rock cliff when teen-agers were soaring past you in chairlifts on their effortless way to the top and giggling at the anachronist who wanted to do it the hard way!

Some of the nearer slopes were blackened with the scars of old forest-fires, and he estimated that the clearing where the ship lay was second-growth from some such fire a few years before. Lucky the ship's fire-prevention systems had prevented any fire on impact—otherwise if anyone had escaped alive, it might have been quite literally from a frying pan into a raging forest fire. They'd have to be careful in the woods. Earth people had lost their old woodcraft habits and might not be aware any more of what forest fires could do. He made a mental note of it for his report.

As he re-entered the area of the crash, his brief euphoria vanished. Inside the field hospital, through the semi-transparent plastic of the shelter material, he could see rows and rows of unconscious or semiconscious bodies. A group of men were trimming branches from treetrunks and another small group was raising a dymaxion dome— the kind, based on triangular bracings, which could be built in half a day. He began to wonder what the report of the Engineering crew had been. He could see a crew of machinists crawling around on the crumpled bracings of the starship, but it didn't look as if much had been accomplished. In fact, it didn't look hopeful for getting away very soon.

As he passed the hospital, a young man in a stained and crumpled Medic uniform came out and called.

"Rafe! The Mate said report to the First Dome as soon as you get back—there's a meeting there and they want you. I'm going over there myself for a Medic report —I'm the most senior man they can spare." He moved slowly beside MacAran. He was slight and small, with light-brown hair and a small curly brown beard, and he looked weary, as if he had had no sleep. MacAran asked, hesitatingly, "How are things going in the hospital?"

"Well, no more deaths since midnight, and we've taken

four more people off critical. There evidently wasn't a leak in the atomics after all—that girl from Comm checked out with no radiation burns; the vomiting was evidently just a bad blow in the solar plexus. Thank God for small favors—if the atomics had sprung a leak, we'd probably all be dead, and another planet contaminated."

"Yeah, the M-AM drives have saved a lot of lives," MacAran said. "You look awfully tired, Ewen—have you had any sleep at all?"

Ewen Ross shook his head. "No, but the Old Man's been generous with wakers, and I'm still racing my motors. About midafternoon I'm probably going to crash and I won't wake up for three days, but until then I'm holding on." He hesitated, looked shyly at his friend and said, "I heard about Jenny, Rafe. Tough luck. So many of the girls back in that area made it out, I was sure she was okay."

"So was I." MacAran drew a deep breath and felt the clean air like a great weight on his chest. "I haven't seen Heather—is she—"

"Heather's okay; they drafted her for nursing duty. Not a scratch on her. I understand after this meeting they're going to post completed lists of the dead, the wounded and the survivors. What were you doing, anyway? Del Rey told me you'd been sent out, but I didn't know what for."

"Preliminary surveying," MacAran said. "We have no idea of our latitude, no idea of the planet's size or mass, no idea about climate or seasons or what have you. But I've established that we can't be too far off the equator, and—well, I'll be making the report inside. Do we go right in?"

"Yeah, in the First Dome." Half unconsciously, Ewen had spoken the words with capital letters, and MacAran thought how human a trait it was to establish location and orientation at once. Three days they had been here and already this first shelter was the First Dome, and the field shelter for the wounded was the Hospital.

There were no seats inside the plastic dome, but some canvas groundsheets and empty supply boxes had been set around and someone had brought a folding chair down for Captain Leicester. Next to him, Camilla Del Rey sat on a box with a lapboard and notebook on her knees; a tall, slender, dark-haired girl with a long, jagged cut across her

10

cheek, mended with plastic clips. She was wrapped in the warm fatigue uniform of a crewmember, but she had shucked the heavy parka-like top and wore only a thin, clinging cotton shirt beneath it. MacAran shifted his eyes from her, quickly—*damn it, what was she up to, sitting around in what amounted to her underwear in front of half the crew! At a time like this it wasn't decent . . .* then, looking at the girl's drawn and wounded face, he absolved her. She was hot—it *was* hot in here now—and she was, after all, on duty, and had a right to be comfortable.

If anyone's out of line it's me, eying a girl like this at a time like this. . . .

Stress. That's all it is. There are too damn many things it's not safe to remember or think about. . . .

Captain Leicester raised his grey head. *He looks like death,* MacAran thought, *probably he hasn't slept since the crash either.* He asked the Del Rey girl, "Is that everyone?"

"I think so."

The Captain said, "Ladies, gentlemen. We won't waste time on formalities, and for the duration of this emergency the protocols of etiquette are suspended. Since my recording officer is in the hospital, Officer Del Rey has kindly agreed to act as communications recorder for this meeting. First of all; I have called you together, a representative from every group, so that each of you can speak to your crews with authority about what is happening and we can minimize the growth of rumors and uninformed gossip about our position. And anywhere that more than twenty-five people are gathered, as I remember from my Pensacola days, rumors and gossip start up. So let's get your information here, and not rely on what somebody told someone else's best friend a few hours ago and what somebody else heard in the mess room—all right? Engineering; let's begin with you. What's the situation with the drives?"

The Chief Engineer—his name was Patrick, but MacAran didn't know him personally—stood up. He was a lanky gaunt man who resembled the folk hero Lincoln. "Bad," he said laconically. "I'm not saying they can't be fixed, but the whole drive room is a shambles. Give us a week to sort it out, and we can estimate how long it will take to fix the drives. Once the mess is cleared away, I'd say—three weeks to a month. But I'd hate to have my year's salary depend on how close I came inside that estimate."

Leicester said, "But it *can* be fixed? It's not hopelessly wrecked?"

"I wouldn't think so," Patrick said. "Hell, it better *not* be! We may need to prospect for fuels, but with the big converter that's no problem, any kind of hydrocarbon will do—even cellulose. That's for energy-conversion in the life-support system, of course; the drive itself works on anti-matter implosions." He became more technical, but before MacAran got too hopelessly lost, Leicester stopped him.

"Save it, Chief. The important thing is, you're saying *it can be fixed,* preliminary estimated time three to six weeks. Officer Del Rey, what's the status on the bridge?"

"Mechanics are in there now, Captain, they're using cutting torches to get out the crumpled metal. The computer console is a mess, but the main banks are all right, and so is the library system."

"What's the worst damage there?"

"We'll need new seats and straps all through the bridge cabin—the mechanics can handle that. And of course we'll have to re-program our destination from the new location, but once we find out exactly where we are, that should be simple enough from the Navigation systems."

"Then there's nothing hopeless there either?"

"It's honestly too early to say, Captain, but I shouldn't think so. Maybe it's wishful thinking, but I haven't given up yet."

Captain Leicester said, "Well, just now things look about as bad as they can; I suspect we're all tending to look on the grim side. Maybe that's good; anything better than the worst will be a pleasant surprise. Where's Dr. Di Asturien? Medic?"

Ewen Ross stood up. "The Chief didn't feel he could leave, sir; he's got a crew working to salvage all remaining medical supplies. He sent me. There have been no more deaths and all the dead are buried. So far there is no sign of any unusual illness of unknown origin, but we are still checking air and soil samples, and will continue to do so, for the purpose of classifying known and unknown bacteria. Also—"

"Go on."

"The Chief wants orders issued about using only the assigned latrine areas, Captain. He pointed out that we're carrying all sorts of bacteria in our own bodies which might damage the local flora and fauna, and we can manage to disinfect the latrine areas fairly thoroughly—but we should take precautions against infecting outside areas."

"A good point," Leicester said. "Ask someone to have the orders posted, Del Rey. And put a security man to make sure everybody knows where the latrines are, and uses them. No taking a leak in the woods just because you're there and there aren't any anti-littering laws."

Camilla Del Rey said, "Suggestion, Captain. Ask the cooks to do the same with the garbage, for a while, anyhow."

"Disinfect it? Good point. Lovat, what's the status on the food synthesizer?"

"Accessible and working, sir, at least temporarily. It might not be a bad idea, though, to check indigenous food supplies and make sure we *can* eat the local fruits and roots if we have to. If it goes on the blink—and it was never intended to run for long periods in planetary gravities—it will be too late to start testing the local vegetation *then*." Judith Lovat, a small, sturdily built woman in her late thirties with the green emblem of Life-support systems on her smock, glanced toward the door of the dome. "The planet seems to be widely forested; there should be something we can eat, with the oxygen-nitrogen system of this air. Chlorophyll and photosynthesis seem to be pretty much the same on all M-type planets and the end product is usually some form of carbohydrate with amino acids."

"I'm going to put a botanist right on it," Captain Leicester said, "which brings me to you, MacAran. Did you get any useful information from the hilltop?"

MacAran stood up. He said, "I would have gotten more if we'd landed in the plains—assuming there are any on this planet—but I did get a few things. First, we're about a thousand feet above sea level here, and definitely in the Northern hemisphere, but not too many degrees of latitude off the Equator, considering that the Sun runs high in the sky. We seem to be in the foothills of an enormous mountain range, and the mountains are old enough to be forested—that is, no active apparent volcanoes in sight, and no mountains which look like the result of volcanic activity within the last few millennia. It's not a young planet."

"Signs of life?" Leicester asked.

"Birds in plenty. Small animals, perhaps mammals but I'm not sure. More kinds of trees than I knew how to identify. A good many of them were a kind of conifer, but there seemed to be hardwoods too, of a kind, and some bushes with various seeds and things. A botanist could tell you a lot more. No signs of any kind of artifact, however, no signs that anything has ever been cultivated or touched. As far as I can tell, the planet's untouched by human—or any other—hands. But of course we may be in the middle of the equivalent of the Siberian steppes or the Gobi desert—way, way off the beaten track."

He paused, then said, "About twenty miles due east of here, there's a prominent mountain peak—you can't miss it—from which we could take sightings, and get some rough estimate of the planet's mass, even without elaborate instruments. We might also sight for rivers, plains, water supply, or any signs of civilization."

Camilla Del Rey said, "From space there was no sign of life."

Moray, the heavy swarthy man who was the official representative of Earth Expeditionary, and in charge of the Colonists, said quietly, "Don't you mean no signs of a technological civilization, Officer? Remember, until a scant four centuries ago, a starship approaching Earth could not have seen any signs of intelligent life there, either."

Captain Leicester said curtly, "Even if there is some form of pre-technological civilization, that is equivalent to no civilization at all, and whatever form of life there may be here, sapient or not, is not of any consequences to our purpose. They could give us no help in repairing our ship, and provided we are careful not to contaminate their ecosystems, there is no reason to approach them and create culture shock."

"I agree with your last statement," Moray said slowly, "but I would like to raise one question you have not yet mentioned, Captain. Permission?"

Leicester grunted, "First thing I said was that we're suspending protocol for the duration—go ahead."

"What's being done to check this planet out for habit-

14

ability, in the event the drives *can't* be repaired, and we're stuck here?"

MacAran felt a moment of shock which stopped him cold, then a small surge of relief. Someone had said it. Someone else was thinking about it. He hadn't had to be the one to bring it up.

But on Captain Leicester's face the shock had not gone away; it had frozen into a stiff cold anger. "There's very little chance of that."

Moray got heavily to his feet. "Yes. I heard what your crew was saying, but I'm not entirely convinced. I think that we should start, at once, to take inventory of what we have, and what is here, in the event that we are marooned here permanently."

"Impossible," Captain Leicester said harshly. "Are you trying to say you know more than my crew about the condition of our ship, Mr. Moray?"

"No. I don't know a damn thing about starships, don't know as I particularly want to. But I know *wreckage* when I see it. I know a good third of your crew is dead, including some important technicians. I heard officer Del Rey say that she thought—she only *thought*—that the navigational computer could be fixed, and I do know that nobody can navigate a M-AM drive in interstellar space without a computer. We've got to take it into account that this ship may not be going *anywhere*. And in that case, we won't be going anywhere either. Unless we've got some boy genius who can build an interstellar communications satellite in the next five years with the local raw materials and the handful of people we have here, and send a message back to Earth, or to the Alpha Centauri or Coronis colonies to come and fetch their little lost sheep."

Camilla Del Rey said in a low voice, "Just what are you trying to do, Mr. Moray? Demoralize us further? Frighten us?"

"No. I'm trying to be realistic."

Leicester said, making a noble effort to control the fury that congested his face, "I think you're out of order, Mr. Moray. Our first order of business is to repair the ship, and for that purpose it may be necessary to draft every man, *including* the passengers from your Colonists group. We cannot spare large groups of men for remote contingencies," he added emphatically, "so if

15

that was a request, consider it denied. Is there any other business?"

Moray did not sit down. "What happens then if six weeks from now we discover that you *can't* fix your ship? Or six months?"

Leicester drew a deep breath. MacAran could see the desperate weariness in his face and his effort not to betray it. "I suggest we cross that bridge if, and when, we see it in the distance, Mr. Moray. There is a very old proverb that says, sufficient unto the day is the evil thereof. I don't believe that a delay of six weeks will make all that difference in resigning ourselves to hopelessness and death. As for me, I intend to live, and to take this ship home again, and anyone who starts defeatist talk will have to reckon with me. Do I make myself clear?"

Moray was evidently not satisfied; but something, perhaps only the Captain's will, kept him quiet. He lowered himself into his seat, still scowling.

Leicester pulled Camilla's lapboard toward him. "Is there anything else? Very well. I believe that will be all, ladies and gentlemen. Lists of survivors and wounded, and their condition, will be posted tonight. Yes, Father Valentine?"

"Sir, I have been requested to say a Requiem Mass for the dead, at the site of the mass graves. Since the Protestant chaplain was killed in the crash, I would like to offer my services to anyone, of any faith, who can use them for anything whatsoever."

Captain Leicester's face softened as he looked at the young priest, his arm in a sling and one side of his face heavily bandaged. He said, "Hold your service by all means, Father. I suggest dawn tomorrow. Find someone who can work on erecting a suitable memorial here; some day, maybe a few hundred years from now, this planet may be colonized, and they should know. We'll have time for that, I imagine."

"Thank you, Captain. Will you excuse me? I must go back to the hospital."

"Yes, Father, go ahead. Anyone who wants to get back now is excused—unless there are any questions? Very well." Leicester leaned back in his seat and closed his eyes briefly. "MacAran and Dr. Lovat, will you stay a minute, please?"

MacAran came forward slowly, surprised beyond

16

words; he had never spoken to the Captain before, and had not realized that Leicester knew him even by sight. What could he want? The others were leaving the dome, one by one; Ewen touched his shoulder briefly and whispered, "Heather and I will be at the Requiem Mass, Rafe. I've got to go. Come around to the hospital and let me check that concussion. Peace, Rafe; see you later," before he slipped away.

Captain Leicester had slumped in his chair, and he looked exhausted and old, but he straightened slightly as Judith Lovat and MacAran approached him. He said, "MacAran, your profile said you've had some mountain experience. What's your professional specialty?"

"Geology. It's true, I've spent a good deal of time in the mountains."

"Then I'm putting you in charge of a brief survey expedition. Go climb that mountain, if you can get up it, and take your sights from the peak, estimate the planet's mass, and so forth. Is there a meteorologist or weather specialist in the colonist group?"

"I suppose so, sir. Mr. Moray would know for sure."

"He probably would, and it might be a good idea for me to make a point of asking him," Leicester said. He was so weary he was almost mumbling. "If we can estimate what the weather in the next few weeks is likely to do, we can decide how best to provide shelter and so forth for the people. Also, any information about period of rotation, and so forth, might be worth something to Earth Expeditionary. And—Dr. Lovat—locate a zoologist and a botanist, preferably from the colonists, and send them along with MacAran. Just in case the food synthesizers break down. They can make tests and take samples."

Judith said, "May I suggest a bacteriologist too, if there's one available?"

"Good idea. Don't let repair crews go short, but take what you need, MacAran. Anyone else you want to take along?"

"A medical technician, or at least a medical nurse," MacAran requested, "in case somebody falls down a crevasse or gets chewed up by the local equivalent of *Tyrannosaurus Rex*."

"Or picks up some ghastly local bug," Judith said. "I ought to have thought of that."

"Okay, then, if the Medic chief can spare anybody,"

17

Leicester agreed. "One more thing. First Officer Del Rey is going with you."

"May I ask what for?" MacAran said, slightly startled. "Not that she isn't welcome, though it might be a rough trek for a lady. This isn't Earth and those mountains haven't any chairlifts!"

Camilla's voice was low and slightly husky. He wondered if it was grief and shock, or whether that was her natural tone. She said, "Captain, MacAran evidently doesn't know the worst of it. How much do you know about the crash and its cause, then?"

He shrugged. "Rumors and the usual gossip. All I know is that the alarm bells began to ring, I got to a safety area—so-called," he added, bitterly, remembering Jenny's mangled body, "and the next thing I knew I was being dragged out of the cabin and hauled down a ladder. Period."

"Well, then, here it is. We don't know where we are. We don't know what Sun this is. We don't know even approximately what star cluster we're in. We were thrown off course by a gravitational storm—that's the layman's term, I won't bother explaining what causes it. We lost our orientation equipment with the first shock, and we had to locate the nearest star-system with a potentially habitable planet, and get down in a hurry. So I've got to take some astronomical sightings, if I can, and locate some known stars—I can do that with spectroscopic readings. From there I may be able to triangulate our position in the Galactic Arm, and do at least part of the computer re-programming from the planet's surface. It is easier to take astronomical observations at an altitude where the air is thinner. Even if I don't get to the mountain's peak, every additional thousand feet of altitude will give me a better chance for accurate readings." The girl looked serious and grave, and he sensed that she was holding fear at bay with her deliberately didactic and professional manner. "So if you can have me along on your expedition, I'm strong and fit, and I'm not afraid of a long hard march. I'd send my assistant, but he has burns over 30 per cent of his body surface and even if he recovers—and it's not certain he will—he won't be going anywhere for a long, long time. There's no one else who knows as much about navigation and Galactic Geography as I do, I'm afraid, so I'd trust my own readings more than anyone else's."

18

MacAran shrugged. He was no male chauvinist, and if the girl thought she could handle the expedition's long marches, she could probably do it. "Okay," he said, "it's up to you. We'll need rations for four days minimum, and if your equipment is heavy, you'd better arrange to have someone else carry it; everybody else will have his own scientific paraphernalia." He looked at the thin shirt clinging damply to her upper body and added, a little harshly, "Dress warmly enough, damn it; you'll get pneumonia."

She looked startled, confused, then suddenly angry; her eyes snapped at him, but MacAran had already forgotten her. He said to the Captain, "When do you want us to start? Tomorrow?"

"No, too many of us haven't had enough sleep," said Leicester, dragging himself up again from what looked like a painful doze. "Look who's talking—and half my crew are in the same shape. I'm going to order everybody but half a dozen watchmen to sleep tonight. Tomorrow, except for basic work crews, we'll dismiss everyone for the memorial services for the dead; and there's a lot of inventorying to do, and salvage work. Start—oh, two, three days from now. Any preference about a medical officer?"

"May I have Ewen Ross if the chief can spare him?"

"It's okay by me," Leicester said, and sagged again, evidently for a split second asleep where he sat. MacAran said a soft, "Thank you, sir," and turned away. Camilla Del Rey laid a hand, a feather's touch, on his arm.

"Don't you dare judge him," she said in a low, furious voice, "he's been on his feet since two days before the crash on a steady diet of wakers, and he's too old for that! I'm going to see he gets 24 hours straight sleep if I have to shut down the whole camp!"

Leicester pulled himself up again. "—wasn't asleep," he said firmly. "Anything else, MacAran, Lovat?"

MacAran said a respectful, "No, sir," and slipped quietly away, leaving the Captain to his rest, his First Officer standing over him like—the image touched his mind in shock—a fiercely maternal tiger over her cub. *Or over the old lion?* And why did he care anyhow?

Chapter
TWO

Too much of the passenger section was either flooded with fire-prevention foam, or oil-slick and dangerous; for that reason, Captain Leicester had given orders that all members of the expedition to the mountain were to be issued surface uniform, the warm, weatherproof garments meant for spaceship personnel to wear on visiting the surface of an alien planet. They had been told to be ready just after sunrise, and they were ready, shouldering their rucksacks of rations, scientific equipment, makeshift campout gear. MacAran stood waiting for Camilla Del Rey, who was giving final instructions to a crewman from the bridge.

"These times for sunrise and sunset are as exact as we can get them, and you have exact azimuth readings for the direction of sunrise. We may have to estimate noon. But every night, at sunset, shine the strongest light in the ship in this direction, and leave it on for exactly ten minutes. That way we can run a line of direction to where we're going, and establish due east and west. You already know about the noon angle readings."

She turned and saw MacAran standing behind her. She said, with composure, "Am I keeping you waiting? I'm sorry, but you must understand the necessity for accurate readings."

"I couldn't agree more," MacAran said, "and why ask me? You outrank everybody in this party, don't you, ma'am?"

She lifted her delicate eyebrows at him. "Oh, is *that* what's worrying you? As a matter of fact, no. Only on the bridge. Captain Leicester put *you* in charge of this party, and believe me, I'm quite content with that. I probably know as much about mountaineering as you do about celestial navigation—if as much. I grew up in the Alpha colony, and you know what the deserts are like there."

MacAran felt considerably relieved—and perversely annoyed. This woman was just too damned perceptive! Oh, yes, it would minimize tensions if he didn't have to ask her as a superior officer to pass along any orders—or suggestions—about the trip. But the fact remained that somehow she'd managed to make him feel officious, blundering, and like a damn fool!

"Well," he said, "any time you're ready. We've got a good long way to go, over some fairly rough ground. So let's get this show on the road."

He moved away toward where the rest of the group stood gathered, mentally taking stock. Ewen Ross was carrying a good part of Camilla Del Rey's astronomical equipment, since, as he admitted, his medical kit was only a light weight. Heather Stuart, wrapped like the others in surface uniform, was talking to him in low tones, and MacAran thought wryly that it must be love, when your girl got up at this unholy hour to see you off. Dr. Judith Lovat, short and sturdy, had an assortment of small sample cases buckled together over her shoulder. He did not know the other two who were waiting in uniform, and before they moved off, he walked around to face them.

"We've seen each other in the recreation rooms, but I don't think I know you. You are—"

The first man, a tall, hawk-nosed, swarthy man in his middle thirties, said, "Marco Zabal. Xenobotanist. I'm coming at Dr. Lovat's request. I'm used to mountains. I grew up in the Basque country, and I've been on expeditions to the Himalayas."

"Glad to have you." MacAran shook his hand. It would help to have someone else along who knew mountains. "And you?"

"Lewis MacLeod. Zoologist, veterinary specialist."

"Crew member or colonist?"

"Colonist." MacLeod grinned briefly. He was small, fat, and fair-skinned. "And before you ask, no, no formal mountaineering experience—but I grew up in the Scottish Highlands, and even in this day and age, you still have to walk a good ways to get anywhere, and there's more vertical country around than horizontal."

MacAran said, "Well, that's a help. And now that we're all together—Ewen, kiss your girl goodbye and let's get moving."

Heather laughed softly, turning and putting back the hood of the uniform—she was a small girl, slight and delicately made, and she looked even smaller in some larger woman's uniform—"Come off it, Rafe. I'm going with you. I'm a graduate microbiologist, and I'm here to collect samples for the Medic Chief."

"But—" MacAran frowned in confusion. He could understand why Camilla had to come—she was better qualified for the job than any man. And Dr. Lovat, perhaps, understandably felt concerned. He said, "I asked for men on this trip. It's some mighty rough ground." He looked at Ewen for support, but the younger man only laughed.

"Do I have to read you the Terran Bill of Rights? *No law shall be made or formulated abridging the rights of any human being to equal work regardless of racial origin, religion or sex—*"

"Oh, damn it, don't you spout Article Four at me," MacAran muttered. "If Heather wants to wear out her shoe leather and you want to let her, who am I to argue the point?" He still suspected Ewen of arranging it. Hell of a way to start a trip! And here he'd been, despite the serious purpose of this mission, excited about actually having a chance to climb an unexplored mountain—only to discover that he had to drag along, not only a female crew member—who at least looked hardy and in good training—but Dr. Lovat, who might not be old but certainly wasn't as young and vigorous as he could have wished, and the delicate-looking Heather. He said, "Well, let's get going," and hoped he didn't sound as glum as he felt.

He lined them up, leading the way, placing Dr. Lovat and Heather immediately behind him with Ewen so that he would know if the pace he set was too hard for them, Camilla next with MacLeod, and the mountain-trained Zabal to bring up the rear. As they moved away from the ship and through the small clutter of roughly-made buildings and shelters, the great red sun began to lift above the line of faraway hills, like an enormous, inflamed, bloodshot eye. Fog lay thick in the bowl of land where the ship lay, but as they began to climb up out of the valley it thinned and shredded, and in spite of himself, MacAran's spirits began to lift. It was, after all, no small thing to be leading a party of exploration, perhaps the only party of exploration for hundreds of years, on a wholly new planet.

They walked in silence; there was plenty to see. As they reached the lip of the valley, MacAran paused and waited for them to come up with him.

"I have very little experience with alien planets," he said. "But don't blunder into any strange underbrush, look where you step, and I hope I don't have to warn you not to drink the water or eat anything until Dr. Lovat has given it her personal okay. You two are the specialists—" he indicated Zabal and MacLeod, "anything to add to that?"

"Just general caution," MacLeod said. "For all we know this planet could be alive with poisonous snakes and reptiles, but our surface uniforms will protect us against most dangers we can't see. I have a handgun for use in extreme emergencies—if a dinosaur or huge carnivore comes along and rushes us—but in general it would be better to run away than shoot. Remember this is preliminary observation, and don't get carried away in classifying and sampling—the next team that comes here can do that."

"If there is a next team," Camilla murmured. She had spoken under her breath, but Rafael heard her and gave her a sharp look. All he said was, "Everybody, take a compass reading for the peak, and be sure to mark every time we move off that reading because of rough ground. We can see the peak from here; once we get further into the foothills we may not be able to see anything but the next hilltop, or the trees."

At first it was easy, pleasant walking, up gentle slopes between tall, deeply rooted coniferous trunks, surprisingly small in diameter for their height, with long blue-green needles on their narrow branches. Except for the dimness of the red sun, they might have been in a forest preserve on Earth. Now and again Marco Zabal fell out of line briefly to inspect some tree or leaf or root pattern; and once a small animal scooted away in the woods. Lewis MacLeod watched it regretfully and said to Dr. Lovat, "One thing—there are furred mammals here. Probably marsupials, but I'm not sure."

The woman said, "I thought you were going to take specimens."

"I will, on the way back. I've no way to keep live

specimens on the way, how would I know what to feed them? But if you're worried about food supply, I should say that so far every mammal on any planet, without exception, has proved to be edible and wholesome. Some aren't very tasty, but milk-secreting animals are all evidently alike in body chemistry."

Judith Lovat noted that the fat little zoologist was puffing with effort, but she said nothing. She could understand perfectly well the fascination of being the first to see and classify the wildlife of a completely strange planet, a job usually left to highly specialized First Landing teams, and she supposed MacAran wouldn't have accepted him for the trip unless he was physically capable of it.

The same thought was on Ewen Ross's mind as he walked beside Heather, neither of them wasting their breath in talk. He thought, Rafe isn't setting a very hard pace, but just the same I'm not too sure how the women will take it. When MacAran called a halt, a little more than an hour after they had set out, he left the girl and moved over to MacAran's side.

"Tell me, Rafe, how high is this peak?"

"No way of telling, as far off as I saw it, but I'd estimate eighteen-twenty thousand feet."

Ewen asked, "Think the women can handle it?"

"Camilla will have to; she's got to take astronomical observations. Zabal and I can help her if we have to, and the rest of you can stay further down on the slopes if you can't make it."

"I can make it," Ewen said, "Remember, the oxygen content of this air is higher than earth's; anoxia won't set in quite so low." He looked around the group of men and women, seated and resting, except for Heather Stuart, who was digging out a soil sample and putting it into one of her tubes. And Lewis MacLeod had flung himself down full length and was breathing hard, eyes closed. Ewen looked at him with some disquiet, his trained eyes spotting what even Judith Lovat had not seen, but he did not speak. He couldn't order the man sent back at this distance—not alone, in any case.

It seemed to the young doctor that MacAran was following his thoughts when the other man said abruptly, "Doesn't this seem almost too easy, too good? There has to be a catch to this planet *somewhere.* It's too much like a picnic in a forest preserve."

Ewen thought, *some picnic, with fifty-odd dead and over a hundred hurt in the crash,* but he didn't say it, remembering Rafe had lost his sister. "Why not, Rafe? Is there some law that says an unexplored planet *has* to be dangerous? Maybe we're just so conditioned to a life on Earth without risks that we're afraid to step one inch outside our nice, safe technology." He smiled. "Haven't I heard you bitching because on Earth you said that all the mountains, and even the ski slopes, were so smoothed out there wasn't any sense of personal conquest? Not that I'd know—I never went in for danger sports."

"You may have something there," MacAran said, but he still looked somber. "If that's so, though, why do they make such a fuss about First Landing teams when they send them to a new planet?"

"Search me. But maybe on a planet where man never developed, his natural enemies didn't develop either?"

It should have comforted MacAran, but instead he felt a cold chill. If man didn't *belong* here, could he *survive* here? But he didn't say it. "Better get moving again. We've got a long way to go, and I'd like to get on the slopes before dark."

He stopped by McLeod as the older man struggled to his feet. "You all right, Dr. MacLeod?"

"Mac," the older man said with a faint smile, "we're not under ship discipline now. Yes, I'm fine."

"You're the animal specialist. Any theories why we haven't seen anything larger than a squirrel?"

"Two," MacLeod said with a round grin, "the first, of course, being that there aren't any. The second, the one I'm committed to, is that with six, no, seven of us crashing along through the underbrush this way, anything with a brain bigger than a squirrel's keeps a good long way off!"

MacAran chuckled, even while he revised his opinion of the fat little man upward by a good many notches. "Should we try to be quieter?"

"Don't see how we can manage it. Tonight will be a better test. Larger carnivores—if there's any analogy to Earth—will come out then, hoping to catch their natural prey sleeping."

MacAran said, "Then we'd better make it our business

25

that we don't get crunched up by mistake," but as he watched the others sling their packs and get into formation, he thought silently that this was one thing he had forgotten. It was true; the overwhelming attention to safety on Earth had virtually eliminated all but man-made dangers. Even jungle safaris were undertaken in glass-sided trucks, and it wouldn't have occurred to him that night would be dangerous in that way.

They had walked another forty minutes, through thickening trees and somewhat heavier underbrush, where they had to push branches aside, when Judith stopped, rubbing her eyes painfully. At about the same time, Heather lifted her hands and stared at them in horror; Ewen, at her side, was instantly alert.

"What's wrong?"

"My hands—" Heather held them up, her face white. Ewen called, "Rafe, hold up a minute," and the straggling line came to a halt. He took Heather's slim fingers gingerly between his own, carefully examining the erupting greenish dots; behind him Camilla cried out:

"Judy! Oh, God, look at her face!"

Ewen swung around to Dr. Lovat. Her cheeks and eyelids were covered with the greenish dots, which seemed to spread and enlarge and swell as he looked at them. She squeezed her eyes shut. Camilla caught her hands gently as she raised them to her face.

"Don't touch your face, Judy—Dr. Ross, what is it?"

"How the hell do I know?" Ewen looked around as the others gathered around them.

"Anybody else turning green?" He added, "All right, then. This is what I'm here for, and everybody else keep your distance until we know just what we've got. Heather!" He shook her shoulder sharply. "Stop that! You're not going to drop dead, as far as I can tell your vital signs are all just fine."

With an effort, the girl controlled herself. "Sorry."

"Now. Exactly what do you feel? Do those spots hurt?"

"No, dammit, they *itch!*" She was flushed, her face red, her copper hair falling loose around her shoulders; she raised a hand to brush it back, and Ewen caught her wrist, careful to touch only her uniform sleeve. "No, don't touch your face," he said, "that's what Dr. Lovat did. Dr. Lovat, how do you feel?"

"Not so good," she said with some effort, "My face burns, and my eyes—well, you can see."

"Indeed I can." Ewen realized that the lids were swelling and turning greenish; she looked grotesque.

Secretly Ewen wondered if he looked as frightened as he felt. Like everyone there, he had been brought up on stories of exotic plagues to be found on strange worlds. But he was a doctor and this was his job. He said, making his voice as firm as he could, "All right, everyone else stand back; but don't panic, if it was an airborne plague we'd all have caught it, and probably the night we landed here. Dr. Lovat, any other symptoms?"

Judy said, trying to smile, "None—except I'm scared."

Ewen said, "We won't count that—yet." Pulling rubber gloves from a steri-pac in his kit, he quickly took her pulse. "No tachycardia, no depressed breathing. You, Heather?"

"I'm fine, except for the damned itching."

Ewen examined the small rash minutely. It was pinpoint at first, but each papule quickly swelled to a vesicle. He said, "Well, let's start eliminating, What did you and Dr. Lovat do that nobody else did?"

"I took soil samples," she said, "looking for soil bacteria and diatoms."

"I was studying some leaves," Judy said, "trying to see if they had a suitable chlorophyll content."

Marco Zabal turned back his uniform cuffs. "I'll play Sherlock Holmes," he said. "There's your answer." He extended his wrists, showing one or two tiny green dots. "Miss Stuart, did you have to move away any leaves to dig up your samples?"

"Why, yes, some flat reddish ones," she said, and he nodded. "There's your answer. Like any good xenobotanist, I handle any plant with gloves until I'm sure what's in it or on it, and I noticed the volatile oil at the time, but took it for granted. Probably some distant relative of urushiol—*rhus toxicodendron*— poison ivy to you. And it's my guess that if it comes out this quickly, it's simple contact dermatitis and there aren't any serious side effects." He grinned, his long narrow face amused. "Try an antihistamine ointment, if you have any, or give Dr. Lovat a shot, since her eyes are swollen so much it's going to be hard for her to see where she's going. And

27

from now on don't go admiring any pretty leaves until I pass on them, all right?"

Ewen followed his instructions, with a relief so great it was almost pain. He felt totally unable to cope with any alien plagues. A massive hypo of antihistamines quickly shrunk Judith Lovat's swollen eyes to normal, although the green color remained. The tall Basque showed them all his specimen leaf, encased in a transparent plastic sample case. "The red menace that turns you green," he said dryly. "Learn to stay away from alien plants, if you can."

MacAran said, "If everyone's all right, let's move along," but as they gathered up their equipment, he felt half sick with relief, and renewed fear. What other dangers could be lurking in an innocent-looking tree or flower? He said half-aloud to Ewen, "I knew this place was too good to be true."

Zabal heard him and chuckled. "My brother was on the First Landing team that went to the Coronis colony. That's one reason I was heading out there. That's the only reason I happen to know all this. The Expedition Force doesn't care to publicize how tricky planets can be, because no one on our nice, safe Earth would dare go out to them. And of course by the time the major colonizing groups get there, like us, the technological crews have removed the obvious dangers and, shall we say, smoothed things down a bit."

"Let's go," MacAran ordered, without answering. This was a wild planet, but what could he do about it? He'd said he wanted to take risks, now he was having his chance.

But they went on without incident, halting near midday to eat lunch from their packs and allow Camilla Del Rey to check her chronometer and come closer to the exact moment of noon. He drew closer to her as she was watching a small pole she had set up in the ground:

"What's the story?"

"The moment when the shadow is shortest is exact noon. So I note the length every two minutes and when it begins to get longer again, noon—the sun exactly on meridian—is in that two-minute period. This is close enough to true local noon for our measurements." She turned to him and asked in a low voice, "Are Heather and Judy really all right?"

"Oh, yes. Ewen's been checking them at every stop. We don't know how long it will take for the color to fade, but they're fine."

"I nearly panicked," she murmured, "Judy Lovat makes me ashamed of myself. She was so calm."

He noticed that imperceptibly the "Lieutenant Del Rey," "Dr. Lovat," "Dr. MacLeod" of the ship—where, after all, you saw only your few intimates except formally—were melting into Camilla, Judy, Mac. He approved. They might be here a long time. He said something like that, then abruptly asked, "Do you have any idea how long we will be here for repairs?"

"None," she said, "but Captain Leicester says—six weeks if we can repair it."

"If?"

"Of course we can repair it," she said suddenly and sharply, and turned away. "We'll have to. We can't stay here."

He wondered if this were fact or optimism, but did not ask. When he spoke next it was to make some banal remark about the quality of the rations they carried and to hope Judy would find some fresh food sources here.

As the sun angled slowly down over the distant ranges, it grew cold again, and a sharp wind sprang up. Camilla looked apprensively at the gathering clouds.

"So much for astronomical observations," she murmured. "Does it rain *every* night on this damnable planet?"

"Seems like it," MacAran said briefly. "Maybe it's a seasonal thing. But every night, so far, at this season at least—hot at noon, cooling down fast, clouds in the afternoon, rain at evening, snow toward midnight. And fog in the morning."

She said, knitting her brows, "From what I've guessed from the time changes—not that five days can tell us much—it's spring; anyhow the days are getting longer, about three minutes each day. The planet seems to have somewhat more tilt than Earth, which would make for violent weather changes. But maybe after the snow clears and before the fog rises, the sky will clear a little. . . ." and fell silent, thinking. MacAran did not disturb her, but as a thin fine drizzle began to fall, began to search for a camping site. They had better get under canvas before it turned into a downpour.

They were on a downslope; below them lay a broad and almost treeless valley, not in their direct path, but pleasant and green, stretching for two or three miles to the south. MacAran looked down at it, calculating the mile or two lost as against the problems of camping under the trees. Evidently these foothills were interspersed with such little valleys, and through this one ran something like a narrow stream of water—a river? A brook? Could it be used to replenish their water supplies? He raised the question, and MacLeod said, "Test the water, sure. But we'll be safer camping here in the middle of the forest."

"Why?"

For answer MacLeod pointed and MacAran made out something that looked like some herd animal. Details were hard to make out, but they were about the size of small ponies. "That's why," MacLeod said. "For all we know they may be peaceful—or even domesticated. And if they're grazing they're not carnivores. But I'd hate to be in their way if they took a notion to stampede in the night. In the trees we can hear things coming."

Judy came and stood beside them. "They might be good to eat. They might even be domesticable, if anyone ever colonizes this planet some day—save the trouble of importing food animals and beasts of burden from Earth."

Watching the slow, flowing movement of the herd over the grey-green turf, MacAran thought it was a tragedy that man could only see animals in terms of his own needs. *But hell, I like a good steak as well as anyone, who am I to preach?* And maybe within a few weeks they would be gone, and the herd animals, whatever they were, could remain unmolested forever.

They set up a camp on the slope in the midst of the drizzle, and Zabal set about making a fire. Camilla said, "I've got to get to the hilltop at sunset and try to find a line of sight to the ship. They're showing lights to establish sightings."

"You couldn't see anything in this rain," MacAran said sharply. "Visibility's about half a mile now. Even a strong light wouldn't show. Get inside the dome, you're drenched!"

She whirled on him. *"Mister* MacAran, need I remind you that I do not take my orders from you? You are in charge of the exploration party—but I'm here on ship's business and I have duties to perform!" She turned away

30

from the small plastic dome-shaped tent and started up the slope. MacAran, cursing all stubborn female officers, started after her.

"Go back," she said sharply, "I've got my instruments, I can manage."

"You just said I'm in charge of this party. All right, damn it, one of *my* orders is that no one goes off alone! *No* one—and that includes the ship's first officer!"

She turned away without speaking again, forging up the slope, hugging her parka hood around her face against the cold, driving rain. It grew heavier as they climbed, and he heard her slip and stumble in the underbrush, even with the strong handlight she carried. Catching up with her, he put a strong hand under her elbow. She moved to shake it off, but he said harshly, "Don't be a fool, Lieutenant! If you break an ankle we'll all have to carry you —or turn back! Two can find a footing, maybe, where one can't. Come on—take my arm." She remained rigid and he snarled, "Damn it, if you were a man I wouldn't *ask* you politely to let me help—I'd *order* it!"

She laughed shortly. "All right," she said, and gripped his elbow, their two handlights playing on the ground for a path. He heard her teeth chattering, but she did not speak a word of complaint. The slope grew steeper, and on the last few yards MacAran had to scramble up ahead of the girl and reach downward to pull her up. She looked round, searching for the direction; pointed where a very faint glimmer of light showed through the blinding rain.

"Could that be it?" she said uncertainly, "The compass direction seems about right."

"If they're using a laser, yes, I suppose it might show this far, even through the rain." The light blotted out, gleamed briefly, was wiped out again, and MacAran swore. "This rain's turning to sleet—come on, let's get down before we have to *slide* down—on ice underfoot!"

It was steep and slippery, and once Camilla lost her footing on the icy leafmold and slid, rolled and floundered to a stop against a great treetrunk; she lay there half-stunned until MacAran, flashing his light around and calling, caught her in his beam. She was gasping and sobbing with the cold, but when he reached a hand to help her up she shook her head and struggled to her feet. "I can manage. But thank you," she added, grudgingly.

31

She felt exhausted, utterly humiliated. She had been trained that it was her duty to work with men as an equal, and in the usual world she knew, a world of buttons to push and machines to run, physical strength was not a factor she had ever had to take into account. She never stopped to reflect that in all her life she had never known any physical effort greater than gymnastics in the exercise room of the ship, or a space station; she felt that she had somehow failed to carry her own weight, she had somehow betrayed her high position. A ship's officer was supposed to be more competent than *any* civilian! She trudged wearily along down the steep slope, setting her feet down with dogged care, and felt the tears of exhaustion and weariness freezing on her cold cheeks.

MacAran, following slowly, was unaware of her inward struggle, but he felt her weariness through her sagging shoulders. After a moment he put his arm around her waist, and said gently, "Like I said before, if you fall again and get hurt badly we'll have to carry you. Don't do that to us, Camilla." He added, hesitatingly, "You'd have let Jenny help you, wouldn't you?"

She did not answer, but she let herself lean on him. He guided her stumbling steps toward the small glow of light through the tent. Somewhere above them, in the thick trees, the harsh call of a night-bird broke through the noise of the beating sleet, but there was no other sound. Even their steps sounded odd and alien here.

Inside the tent MacAran sagged, gratefully taking the plastic cup of boiling tea MacLeod handed him, stepping carefully to where his sleeping bag had been spread beside Ewen's. He sipped at the boiling liquid, brushing ice from his eyelids, hearing Heather and Judy making cooing sounds over Camilla's icy face, bustling around in the cramped quarters and bringing her hot tea, a dry blanket, helping her out of her iced-over parka. Ewen asked, "What's it doing out there—rain? Hail? Sleet?"

"Mixture of all three, I'd guess. We seem to have lucked right into some kind of equinoctial storm, I'd imagine. It *can't* be like this all year round."

"Did you get your readings?" At MacAran's affirmative nod, he said, "One of us should have gone, the Lieutenant's not really up to that kind of climb in this weather. Wonder what made her try?"

MacAran looked across at Camilla, huddled under a

blanket, with Judy drying her wet, tangled hair as she sipped the boiling tea. He said, surprising himself, *"Noblesse oblige."*

Ewen nodded. "I know what you mean. Let me get you some soup. Judy did some great things with the ration. Good to have a food expert along."

They were all exhausted and talked little of what they had seen; the howling of the wind and sleet outside made speech difficult in any case. Within half an hour they had downed their food and crawled into their sleeping bags. Heather snuggled close to Ewen, her head on his shoulder, and MacAran, just beyond them, looked at their joined bodies with a slow, undefined envy. There seemed a closeness there which had little to do with sexuality. It spoke in the way they shifted their weight, almost unconsciously, each to ease and comfort the other. Against his will he thought of the moment when Camilla had let herself rest against him, and smiled wryly in the dark. Of all the women in the ship she was the least likely to be interested in him, and probably the one he disliked most. But damn it, he had to admire her!

He lay awake for a time, listening to the noise of wind in the heavy trees, to the sound of a tree cracking and crashing down somewhere in the storm—*God! If one fell on the tent, we'd all be killed*—to strange sounds which might be animals crashing through the underbrush. After a while, fitfully, he slept, but with one ear open, hearing MacLeod gasping in his sleep and moaning, once hearing Camilla cry out, a nightmarish cry, then fall again into exhausted sleep. Toward morning the storm quieted and the rain ceased and he slept like the dead, hearing only through his sleep the sounds of strange beasts and birds moving in the nighted forest and on the unknown hills.

Chapter
THREE

Some time before dawn he roused, hearing Camilla stirring, and saw across the dark tent that she was struggling into her uniform. He slid quietly from his sleeping bag, and asked softly, "What is it?"

"The rain's stopped and the sky's clear; I want some sky-sightings and spectrograph readings before the fog comes in."

"Right. Need any help?"

"No, Marco can help carry the instruments."

He started to protest, then shrugged and crawled back into his sleeping bag. It wasn't entirely up to him. She knew her business and didn't need his careful watchfulness. She'd made that amply clear.

Some undefined apprehension, however, kept him from sleeping again; he lay in an uneasy doze, hearing around him the noises of the waking forest. Birds called from tree to tree, some harsh and raucous, some soft and chirping. There were small croakings and stirrings in the underbrush, and somewhere a distant sound not unlike the barking of a dog.

And then the silence was shattered by a horrible yell—a shriek of unquestionably human agony, a harsh scream of anguish, repeated twice and breaking off in a ghastly babbling moan, and silence.

MacAran was out of his sleeping bag and out of the tent, half dressed, Ewen less than half a step behind him, and all the others crowding after, sleepy, bewildered, frightened. He ran up the slope toward the sound, hearing Camilla cry out for help.

She had set her equipment in a clearing near the summit, but now it was knocked over; nearby Marco Zabal lay on the ground, writhing and moaning incoherently. He was swollen and his face had a hideous congested look; Camilla was brushing frantically with her gloved

34

hands. Ewen dropped by the writhing man, with a quick demand to Camilla:

"Quick—what happened!"

"Things—like insects," she said, shaking as she held out her hands. On the gloved palm lay a small crushed thing, less than two inches long, with a curved tail like a scorpion and a wicked fang at the front; it was bright orange and green in color. "He stepped on that mound there, and I heard him scream, and then he fell down—"

Ewen had his medical kit out, and was quickly moving his hands over Zabal's heart. He gave quick directions to Heather, who had dropped beside him, to cut away the man's clothes; the wounded man's face was congested and blackening, and his arm swollen immensely. Zabal was unconscious now, moaning deliriously.

A powerful nerve poison, Ewen thought; his heart is slowing down and his breathing depressed. All he could do now was to give the man a powerful stimulant and stand by in case he needed artificial respiration. He didn't even dare give him anything to ease the agony—almost all narcotics were respiratory depressants. He waited, hardly breathing himself, his stethoscope on Zabal's chest, while the man's faltering heart began to beat a little more regularly; he raised his head to look briefly at the mound, to ask Camilla if she had been bitten—she hadn't, although two of the hideous insects had begun to crawl up her arm—and to demand that everybody stay a good long distance from the mound, or anthill, or whatever it was. *Just dumb luck we didn't camp on top of it in the dark! MacAran and Camilla might have stumbled right into it —or maybe they're dormant in snow!*

Time dragged. Zabal began to breathe again more regularly and to moan a little but he did not recover consciousness. The great red sun, dripping fog, slowly lifted itself up over the foothills surrounding them.

Ewen sent Heather back to the tent for the rest of his medical equipment; Judy and MacLeod began to fix some breakfast. Camilla stoically calculated the few astronomical readings she had been able to take before the attack of the scorpion-ants—MacLeod, after examining the dead one, had temporarily christened them that. MacAran came and stood beside the unconscious man and the young doctor who knelt beside him.

"Will he live?"

"I don't know. Probably. I never saw anything like it since I treated my one and only case of rattlesnake bite. But one thing's certain—he won't be going anywhere today, probably not tomorrow either."

MacAran asked, "Shouldn't we carry him down to the tent? Could there be more of those things crawling around?"

"I'd rather not move him now. Maybe in a couple of hours."

MacAran stood, looking down in dismay, at the unconscious man. They shouldn't delay—and yet, their party had been rigidly calculated for size and there was no one to spare to send back to the ship for help. Finally he said, "We've got to go on. Suppose we move Marco back to the tent, when it's safe, and you stay to look after him. The others can do their exploration work here as well as anywhere, check out soil, plant, animal samples. But I have to survey what I can from the peak, and Lieutenant Del Rey has to take her astronomical sightings from as high up as possible. We'll go on ahead, as far as we can. If the peak turns out to be unclimbable we won't try, just take what readings we can and come back."

"Wouldn't it be better to wait and see whether we can go on with you? We don't know what kind of dangers there are in the forests here."

"It's a matter of time," Camilla said tautly. "The sooner we know where we are, the sooner we have a chance—" she didn't finish.

MacAran said, "We don't know. The dangers might even be less for a very small party, even for a single person. It's even odds, either way. I think we're going to have to do it that way."

They arranged it like that, and since in two hours Zabal had shown no signs of recovering consciousness, MacAran and the other two men carried him, on an improvised stretcher, down to the tent. There was some protest about the splitting of the party, but no one seriously disputed it, and MacAran realized that he had already become their leader whose word was law. By the time the red sun stood straight overhead they had divided the packs and were ready to go, with only the small emergency shelter-tent, food for a few days, and Camilla's instruments.

They stood in the shelter tent, looking down at the

36

semi-conscious Zabal. He had begun to stir and moan but showed no other signs of returning consciousness. Mac-Aran felt desperately uneasy about him, but all he could do was leave him in Ewen's hands. After all, the important business here was the preliminary estimate of this planet —and Camilla's observations as to where in the Galaxy they were!

Something was nagging at his mind. Had he forgotten anything? Suddenly Heather Stuart pulled off her uniform coat and drew off the fut-knit jacket she was wearing under it. "Camilla, it's warmer than yours," she said in a low voice, "please wear it. It snows so here. And you're going to be out with only the small shelter!"

Camilla laughed, shaking her head. "It's going to be cold here too."

"But—" Heather's face was taut and drawn. She bit her lip and pleaded, *"Please,* Camilla. Call me a silly fool, if you like. Say I'm having a premonition, but *please* take it!"

"You too?" MacLeod asked dryly. "Better take it, Lieutenant. I thought I was the only one having freaked-out second sight. I've never taken ESP very seriously, but who knows, on a strange planet it just might turn out to be a survival quality. Anyhow, what can you lose to take a few extra warm clothes?"

MacAran realized that the nagging at his mind *had* been somehow concerned with weather. He said, "Take it, Camilla, if it's extra warm. I'll take Zabal's mountain parka, too, it's heavier than mine, and leave mine for him. And some extra sweaters if you have them. Don't deprive yourselves, but it's true that if it snows you will have more shelter than we do, and it sometimes gets pretty cold on the heights." He was looking at Heather and MacLeod curiously; as a general rule he had no faith in what he had heard about ESP, but if two people in the party both felt it, and he too had some inkling of it— well, maybe it was just a matter of unconscious sensory clues, something they couldn't add up consciously. Anyway, you didn't need ESP to predict bad weather on the mountain heights of a strange planet with a freakishly bad climate! "Take all the clothes anyone can spare, and an extra blanket—we have extras," he ordered, "and then let's get going."

While Heather and Judy were packing, he made time for

a word alone with Ewen. "Wait here for at least eight days for us," he said, "and we'll signal every night at sunset if we can. If there's no word or signal by that time, get back to the ship. If we make it back, no sense disturbing everyone else with this—but if something happens to us, you're in charge."

Ewen felt reluctant to see him go. "What shall I do if Zabal dies?"

"Bury him," MacAran said harshly, "what else?" He turned away and motioned to Camilla. "Let's go, Lieutenant."

They strode away from the clearing without looking back, MacAran setting a steady pace, not too fast, not too slow.

As they climbed higher the land changed, the ground under foot becoming less overgrown, with more bare rocks and sparser trees. The slope of the foothills was not acute, but as they neared the crest of the slope where they had camped, MacAran called a halt to rest and swallow a mouthful of rations. From where they stood they could see the small orange square of the shelter tent, only a flyspeck at this height, through the heavy trees.

"How far have we come, MacAran?" the woman asked, putting back the fur-lined hood of her jacket.

"I've no way of knowing. Five, six miles perhaps; about two thousand feet of altitude. Headache?"

"Only a little," the girl lied.

"That's the change in air pressure; you'll get used to it presently," he said. "Good thing we have a fairly gradual rise in land."

"It's hard to realize that's really where we slept last night—so far down," she said a little shakily.

"Over this ridge it will be out of sight. If you want to chicken out, this is your last chance. You could make it down in an hour, maybe two."

She shrugged. "Don't tempt me."

"Are you frightened?"

"Of course. I'm not a fool. But I won't panic, if that's what you mean."

MacAran rose to his feet, swallowing the last of his ration. "Let's go, then. Watch your step—there are rocks above us."

But to his surprise she was sure-footed on the piled rocks near the peak, and he did not need to help her,

38

or hunt for an easier pass. From the top of the hill they could see a long panorama beneath them, behind them; the valley where they had camped, with its long plain, the further valley where the starship lay—although even with his strong binoculars MacAran could only make out a tiny dark streak that *might* be the ship. Easier to see was the ragged clearing where they had cut trees for shelters. Passing the glasses to Camilla, he said, "Man's first mark on a new world."

"And last, I hope," she said. He wanted to ask her, put it up to her straight, *could* the ship be repaired? But that wasn't the time for thinking about that. He said, "There are streams among the rocks, and Judy tested the water days ago. We can probably find all the water we need to refill our canteens, so don't ration yourself too much."

"My throat feels terribly dry. Is it just the altitude?"

"Probably. On Earth we couldn't come much higher than this without oxygen, but this planet has a higher oxygen content." MacAran took one last look at the orange tent below them; stowed the glasses and slung them over his shoulder. "Well, the next peak will be higher. Let's get on, then." She was looking at some small orange flowers that grew in the crannies of the rock. "Better not touch them. Who knows what might bite, here?"

She turned around, a small orange flower in her fingers. "Too late now," she said with wry grin. "If I'm going to drop dead when I pick a flower, better find it out now than later. I'm not so sure I *want* to go on living if it's a planet where I can't *touch* anything." She added, more seriously, "We've got to take some risks, Rafe—and even then, something we never thought of might kill us. Seems to me that all we can do is take the obvious precautions—and then take our chances."

It was the first time since the crash that she had called him by his first name, and unwillingly he softened. He said, "You're right of course; short of going around in space suits we haven't any real protection, so there's no point in being paranoid. If we were a First Landing Team we'd know what risks not to take, but as it is I guess all we can do is take our chances." It was growing hot, and he stripped off his outer layer of clothing. "I wonder how much stock to put in Heather's premonitions of bad weather?"

They started down the other side of the ridge. Halfway

down the slope, after two or three hours of searching for a path, they discovered a small crystal spring gushing from a split rock, and refilled their canteens; the water tasted sweet and pure, and at MacAran's suggestion they followed the stream down; it would certainly take the shortest way.

At dusk heavy clouds began to scud across the lowering sun. They were in a valley, with no chance to signal the ship or the other camp of their party. While they were setting up the tiny shelter-tent, and MacAran was making fire to heat their rations, a thin fine rain began falling; swearing, he moved the small fire under the flap of the tent, trying to shield it a little from the rain. He managed to get water heated, but not hot, before the gusting sleet put it out again, and he gave up and dumped the dried rations into the barely warm water. "Here. Not tasty but edible—and nourishing, I hope."

Camilla made a face when she tasted it, but to his relief said nothing. The sleet whipped around them and they crawled inside and drew the flap tight. Inside there was barely room enough for one of them to lie at full length while the other sat up—the emergency tents were really only meant for one. MacAran started to make some flippant remark about nice cozy quarters, looked at her drawn face and didn't. He only said, as he wriggled out of his storm parka and pack, and started unrolling his sleeping bag, "I hope you don't suffer from claustrophobia."

"I've been a spaceship officer since I was seventeen. How could I get along with claustrophobia?" In the dark he imagined her smile. "On the contrary."

Neither of them had much to say after that. Once she asked into the darkness, "I wonder how Marco is?" but MacAran had no answer for her, and there was no point in thinking how much better this trip would have been with Marco Zabal's knowledge of the high Himalaya. He did ask, once, just before he dropped off to sleep, "Do you want to get up and try for some star-sights before dawn?"

"No. I'll wait for the peak, I guess, if we get that far." Her breathing quieted into soft exhausted sighs and he knew she slept. He lay awake a little, wondering what lay ahead. Outside, the sleet lashed the branches of the trees and there was a rushing sound which might have been wind or some animal making a rush through the undergrowth. He slept lightly, alert for unexpected sounds. Once or twice Camilla cried out in her sleep and he woke, alert and listening. Had she a touch of altitude sickness? Oxygen content or no oxygen content, the peaks were pretty high and each successive one left their general altitude a little higher. Well, she'd get acclimated, or else she wouldn't. Briefly, on the edge of sleep, MacAran reflected that it was the stuff of entertainment-media, a man alone with a beautiful woman on a strange planet full of dangers. He was conscious of wanting her—hell, he was human and male—but in their present circumstances nothing was further from his mind than sex. *Maybe I'm just too civilized.* In the very thought, exhausted by the day's climbing, he fell asleep.

The next three days were replays of that day, except that on the third night they reached a high pass at dusk and the night's rain had not yet begun. Camilla set up her telescope and made a few observations. He could not forbear, as he set up the shelter-tent in the dark, to ask, "Any luck? Where are we, do you know?"

"Not sure. I knew already that this sun is none of the charted ones, and the only constellations I can spot, from central co-ordinates, are all skewed to the left. I suspect we're right out of the Spiral Arm of the Galaxy—note how few stars there are, compared even to Earth, let alone any centrally located colony planet! Oh, we're a good long way from where we were supposed to be going!" Her voice sounded taut and drawn, and as he moved closer he saw in the darkness that there were tears on her cheeks.

He felt a painful urge to comfort her. "Well, at least when we're on our way again, we'll have discovered a new habitable planet. Maybe you'll even get part of the finder's fee."

"But it's so far—" she broke off. "Can we signal the ship?"

"We can try. We're at least eight thousand feet higher than they are; maybe we're in a line-of-sight. Here, take the glasses, see if you can find any sign of a flash. But of course they could be behind some fold of the hills."

He put his arm around her, steadying the glasses. She did not draw away. She said, "Do you have the bearing for the ship?"

He gave it to her; she moved the glasses slightly, com-

41

pass in hand. "I see a light—no, I think it's lightning. Oh, what difference does it make?" Impatiently she put the glasses aside. He could feel her trembling. "You *like* these wide open spaces, don't you?"

"Why, yes," he said, slowly, "I've always loved the mountains. Don't you?"

In the darkness she shook her head. Above them the pale violet light of one of the four small moons gave a faint tremulous quality to the dimness. She said, faintly, "No. I'm afraid of them."

"Afraid?"

"I've been either on a satellite or training ship since I was picked for space at fifteen. You—" her voice wavered, "you get kind of—agoraphobic."

"And you volunteered to come on this trip!" MacAran said, but she mistook his surprise and admiration for criticism. "Who else was there?" she said harshly, turned away and went into the tiny tent.

Once again, after they had swallowed their food—hot tonight, since there was no rain to put out their fire— MacAran lay awake long after the girl slept. Usually at night there was only the sound of blowing rain and creaking, lashing branches; tonight the forest seemed alive with strange sounds and noises, as if, on the rare snowless night, all its unknown life came alive. Once there was a faraway howling that sounded like a tape he had heard, once, on Earth, of the extinct timber wolf; once an almost feline snarl, low and hoarse, and the terrified cry of some small animal, and then silence. And then, toward midnight, there was a high, eerie scream, a long wailing cry that seemed to freeze the very marrow of his bones. It sounded so uncannily like the scream Marco had given when attacked by the scorpion-ants that for a dreaming moment MacAran, shocked awake, started to leap to his feet; then as Camilla, roused by his movement, sat up in fright, it came again, and he realized nothing human could possibly have made it. It was a shrill, ululating cry that went on, higher and higher, into what seemed like ultrasonics; he seemed to hear it long after it had died away.

"What is it?" Camilla whispered, shaking.

"God knows. Some kind of bird or animal, I suppose."

They listened in silence to the ear-shattering scream again. She moved a little closer to him, and murmured, "It sounds as if it were in agony."

"Don't be imaginative. That may be its normal voice, for all we know."

"*Nothing* has a normal voice like that," she said firmly.

"How can we possibly know that?"

"How can you be so matter of fact? Oooh—" she flinched as the long shrilling sound came again. "It seems to freeze the marrow of my bones!"

"Maybe it uses that sound to paralyze its prey," MacAran said. "It scares me too, damn it! If I were on Earth—well, my people were Irish, and I'd imagine the old Arran banshee had come to carry me off!"

"We'll have to name it *banshee,* when we find out what it is," Camilla said, and she wasn't laughing. The hideous sound came again, and she clapped her hands over her ears, screaming, "Stop it! *Stop it!*"

MacAran slapped her, not very hard. "Stop it yourself, damn you! For all we know it might be prowling around outside and big enough to eat up both of us and the tent too! Let's keep quiet and just lie low until it goes away!"

"That's easier said than done," Camilla murmured, and flinched as the eerie banshee cry came again. She crept closer to him in the crowded quarters of the tent and said, in a very small voice, "Would you—hold my hand?"

He searched for her fingers in the dark. They felt cold and stiff, and he began to chafe them softly between his own. She leaned against him, and he bent down and kissed her softly on the temple. "Don't be afraid. The tent's plastic and I doubt if we smell edible. Let's just hope whatever-it-is, the banshee if you like, catches itself a nice dinner soon and shuts up."

The howling scream sounded again, further away this time and without the ghastly bone-chilling quality. He felt the girl sag against his shoulder and eased her down again, letting her head rest against him. "You'd better get some sleep," he said gently.

Her whisper was almost inaudible. "Thanks, Rafe."

After he knew, by the sound of her steady breathing, that she slept again, he leaned over and kissed her softly. This was one hell of a time to start something like that, he told himself, angry at his own reactions, they had a job to do and there was nothing personal about it. Or shouldn't be. But still it was a long time until he slept.

They came out of the tent in the morning to a world

43

transformed. The sky was clear and unstained by cloud or fog, and underfoot the hardy colorless grass had been suddenly carpeted by quick-opening, quick-spreading colored flowers. No biologist, MacAran had seen something like this in deserts and other barren areas and he knew that places with violent climates often developed forms of life which could take advantage of tiny favorable changes in temperature or humidity, however brief. Camilla was enchanted with the multicolored low-growing flowers and with the bee-like creatures who buzzed among them, although she was careful not to disturb them.

MacAran stood surveying the land ahead. Across one more narrow valley, crossed by a small running stream, lay the last slopes of the high peak which was their destination.

"With any luck we should be near the peak tonight, and tomorrow, just at noon, we can take our survey readings. You know the theory—triangulate the distance between here and the ship, calculate the angle of the shadow, we can estimate the size of the planet. Archimedes or somebody like that did it for Earth, thousands of years before anyone ever invented higher mathematics. And if it doesn't rain tonight you may be able to get some clearer sightings from the heights."

She was smiling. "Isn't it wonderful what just a little change in the weather can do? Will it be much of a climb?"

"I don't think so. It looks from here as if we could walk straight up the slope—evidently the timberline on this planet is higher than most worlds. There's bare rock and no trees near the peak, but only a couple of thousand feet below there's vegetation. We haven't reached the snowline yet."

On the higher slopes, in spite of everything, MacAran recovered his old enthusiasm. A strange world perhaps, but still, a mountain beneath him, the challenge of a climb. An easy climb it was true, without rocks or icefalls, but that simply freed him to enjoy the mountain panorama, the high clear air. It was only Camilla's presence, the knowledge that she feared the open heights, that kept him in touch with reality at all. He had expected to resent this, the need to help an amateur over easy stretches which he could have climbed with one leg in a cast, the waiting for her to find footing on the stretches of steep

44

rocky scree, but instead he found himself curiously in rapport with her fear, her slow conquest of each new height. A few feet below the high peak he stopped.

"Here. We can run a perfectly good line of sight from here, and there's a flat spot to set up your equipment. We'll wait here for noon."

He had expected her to show relief; instead she looked at him, with a certain shyness, and said, "I thought you'd like to climb the peak, Rafe. Go ahead, if you want to, I don't mind."

He started to snap at her that it would be no fun at all with a frightened amateur, then realized this was no longer true. He pulled his pack off his shoulder and smiled at her, laying a hand on her arm. "That can wait," he said gently, "this isn't a pleasure trip, Camilla. This is the best spot for what we want to do. Did you adjust your chronometer so that we can catch noon?"

They rested side by side on the slope, looking down across the panorama of forests and hills spread out below them. *Beautiful*, he thought, *a world to love, a world to live in.*

He asked idly, "Do you suppose the Coronis colony is this beautiful?"

"How would I know? I've never been there. Anyway, I don't know all that much about planets. But this one is beautiful. I've never seen a sun quite this color, and the shadows—" she fell silent, staring down at the pattern of greens and dark-violet shade in the valleys.

"It would be easy to get used to a sky this color," MacAran said, and was silent again.

It was not long until the shortening shadows marked the approach of the meridian. After all the preparation, it seemed a curious anticlimax; to unfold the hundred-foot-high aluminum rod, to measure the shadows exactly, to the millimeter. When it was finished and he was re-folding the rod, he said as much, wryly:

"Forty miles and an eighteen-thousand-foot climb for a hundred and twenty seconds of measurements."

Camilla shrugged. "And God-knows-how-many light-years to come here. Science is all like that, Rafe."

"Nothing to do now but wait for the night, so you can take your observations." Rafe folded the rod and sat down on the rocks, enjoying the rare warmth of the sunlight. Camilla went on moving around their campsite for a little, then came back and joined him. He asked, "Do you really think you can chart this planet's position, Camilla?"

"I hope so. I'm going to try and observe known Cepheid variables, take observations over a period of time, and if I can find as many as three that I can absolutely identify, I can compute where we are in relation to the central drift of the Galaxy."

"Let's pray for a few more clear nights, then," Rafe said, and was silent.

After some time, watching him study the rocks less than a hundred feet above them, she said, "Go on, Rafe. You know you want to climb it. Go ahead, I don't mind."

"You don't? You won't mind waiting here?"

"Who said I'd wait here? I think I can make it. And—" she smiled a little, "I suppose I'm as curious as you are —to get one glimpse of what's beyond it!"

He rose with alacrity. "We can leave everything but the canteens here," he said. "It *is* an easy enough climb—not a climb at all, really; just a steep sort of scramble." He felt light-hearted, joyous at her sudden sharing of his mood. He went ahead, searching out the easiest route. showing her where to set her feet. Common sense told him that this climb, based only on curiosity to see what lay beyond and not on their mission's needs, was a little foolhardy—who could risk a broken ankle?—but he could not contain himself. Finally they struggled up the last few feet and stood looking out over the peak. Camilla cried out in surprise and a little dismay. The shoulder of the mountain on which they stood had obscured the real range which lay beyond; an enormous mountain range which lay, seemingly endless and to the very edge of their sight, wrapped in eternal snow, enormous and jagged and covered with glaciated ridges and peaks below which pale clouds drifted, lazily and slow.

Rafe whistled. "Good God, it makes the Himalayas look like foothills," he muttered.

"It seems to go on forever! I suppose we didn't see it before because the air wasn't so clear, with clouds and fog and rain, but—" Camilla shook her head in wonder. "It's like a wall around the world!"

"This explains something else," Rafe said slowly. "The freak weather. Flowing over a series of glaciers like that, no wonder there's almost perpetual rain, fog, snow—you name it! And if they are really as high as they look—I

46

can't tell how far away they are, but they could easily be a hundred miles on a clear day like this—it would also explain the tilt of this world on its axis. They call the Himalayas, on Earth, a third pole. This is a *real* third pole! A third icecap, anyway."

"I'd rather look the other way," Camilla said, and faced back toward the folds and folds of green-violet valleys and forests. "I prefer my planets with trees and flowers—and sunlight, even if the sunlight is the color of blood."

"Let's hope it shows us some stars tonight—and some moons."

Chapter
FOUR

"I simply can't believe this weather," Heather Stuart said, and Ewen, stepping to the door of the tent, jeered gently, "What price your blizzard warnings now?"

"I'm glad to be wrong," Heather said firmly, "Rafe and Camilla need it, on the mountain." An expression of disquiet passed over her face. "I'm not so sure I *was* wrong, though, there's something about this weather that scares me a little. It seems all wrong for this planet somehow."

Ewen chuckled. "Still defending the honor of your old Highland granny and her second-sight?"

Heather did not smile. "I never believed in second sight. Not even in the Highlands. But now I'm not so sure. How is Marco?"

"Not much change, although Judy did manage to get him to swallow a little broth. He seems a little better, although his pulse is still awfully uneven. Where is Judy, by the way?"

"She went into the woods with MacLeod. I made her promise not to go out of sight of the clearing, though." A sound inside of the tent drew them both back; for the first time in three days, something other than inarticulate moans from Zabal. Inside he was moving, struggling to

47

sit up. He muttered, in a hoarse astonished voice, *"Que pasó? O Dio, mi duele—duele tanto—"*

Ewen bent over him, saying gently, "It's all right, Marco, you're here, we're with you. Are you in pain?"

He muttered something in Spanish. Ewen looked blankly up at Heather, who shook her head. "I don't speak it; Camilla does, but I only know a few words." But before she could muster any of them, Zabal muttered, "Pain? You'd better believe! What *were* those things? How long —where's Rafe?"

Ewen checked the man's heart-rate before he spoke. He said, "Don't try to sit up; I'll put a pillow behind your head. You've been very ill; we thought you weren't going to make it." *And I'm still not so sure,* he thought grimly, even while he wadded his spare coat to put behind the injured man's head and Heather encouraged him to swallow some soup. *No, please, there have been too many deaths.* But he knew this would make no difference. On Earth only the old died, as a rule. Here— well, it was different. Damn different.

"Don't waste your breath talking. Save your strength and we'll tell you everything," he said.

The night fell, still miraculously clear and free of fog or rain. Even on the heights, no fog closed in, and Rafe, setting up Camilla's telescope and other instruments on the flat place of their camp, saw for the first time the stars rise over the peaks, clear and brilliant but very far away. He did not know a Cepheid variable from a constellation, so much of what she was trying to do was incomprehensible to him; but with a carefully shielded light—not to spoil the dark-adaptation of her eyes—he wrote down careful strings of figures and co-ordinates as she gave them. After what seemed hours of this, she sighed and stretched cramped muscles.

"That's all I can do for now; I can take more readings just before dawn. Still no sign of rain?"

"None, thank goodness."

Around them the scent from the flowers on the lower slopes was sweet and intoxicating, as quick-blooming shrubs, vivified by two days of heat and dryness, burst and opened all around. The unfamiliar scents were a little dizzying. Over the mountain floated a great gleaming moon, with a pale iridescent glow; then, following it by only a few moments, another, this one with pale violet lustre.

"Look at the moon," she whispered.

"Which moon?" Rafe smiled in the darkness. "Earthmen get used to saying, *the* moon; I suppose some day someone will give them names. . . ."

They sat on the soft dry grass, watching the moons swing free of the mountains and rise. Rafe quoted softly, "If the stars shone only one night in a thousand years, how men would look and wonder and adore."

She nodded. "Even after ten days, I find I miss them."

Rationally Rafe knew that it was madness to sit here in the dark. If nothing else, birds or beasts of prey—perhaps the banshee-screamer from the heights they had heard last night—might be abroad in the dark. He said so, finally, and Camilla, like the breaking of a spell, started and said, "You're right. I must wake well before dawn."

Rafe was somehow reluctant to go into the stuffy darkness of the shelter-tent. He said, "In the old days it used to be believed it was dangerous to sleep in the moonlight—that's where the word lunatic came from. Would it be four times as dangerous to sleep under four moons, I wonder?"

"No, but it would be—lunatic," Camilla said, laughing gently. He stopped, took her shoulders in a gentle grip and for a moment the girl, biting back a tart remark, thought in a mixture of fear and anticipation that he would bend down and kiss her; but then he turned away and said, "Who wants to be sane? Good night, Camilla. See you an hour before sunrise," and strode away, leaving her to go before him into the shelter.

A clear night, over the planet of the four moons. Banshees prowled on the heights, freezing their warm-blooded prey with their screams, blundering toward them by the heat of their blood, but never coming below the snow-line; on a snowless night, anything on rock or grass was safe. Above the valleys, great birds of prey swung; beasts still unknown to the Earthmen prowled in the depths of the deep forest, living and dying, and trees unheard crashed to the ground. Under the moonlight, in the unaccustomed heat and dryness of a warm wind blowing away from the glaciated ridges, flowers bloomed and opened, and shed their perfume and pollen. Night-bloom-

49

ing and strange, with a deep and intoxicating scent. . . .

The red sun rose clear and cloudless, a brilliant sunrise with the sun like a giant ruby in a clear garnet sky. Rafe and Camilla, who had been at the telescope for two hours, sat and watched it with the pleasant fatigue of a light task safely over for some time.

"Shall we start down? This weather is too good to last," Camilla said, "and although I've gotten used to the mountain in the sun, I don't think I'd care to navigate it on ice."

"Right. Pack up the instruments—you know how they go—and I'll fix a bite of rations and strike the tent. We'll start down while the weather holds—not that it doesn't look like a gorgeous day. If it's still fine tonight we can stop on one of the hilltops and camp out, and you can take some more sightings," he said.

Within forty minutes they were going down. Rafe cast a wistful look back at the huge unknown range before turning his back on it. His own undiscovered range, and probably he would never see it again.

Don't be too sure, a voice remarked precisely in his mind, but he shrugged it off. He didn't believe in precognition.

He sniffed the light flower-scents, half enjoying them, half disturbed by their faintly acrid sweetness. The most noticeable were the tiny orange flowers Camilla had plucked the day before, but there was also a lovely white flower, star-shaped with a golden corolla, and a deep blue bell-like blossom with inner stalks covered with a shimmering gold-colored dust. Camilla bent over, inhaling the spicy fragrance. Rafe thought to warn her, after a moment;

"Remember Heather and Judy turning green? Serve you right if you do!"

She looked up, laughing. Her face looked faintly gold from the flower-dust. "If it was going to hurt me it would have already—the air's full of the scent, or haven't you noticed? Oh, it's so beautiful, so beautiful, I feel like a flower myself, I feel as if I could get drunk on flowers—"

She stood rapt, gazing at the beautiful bell-shaped blossom and seeming to shimmer with the golden dust. *Drunk,* Rafe thought, *drunk on flowers.* He let his pack slip from his shoulder and roll away.

"You *are* a flower," he said hoarsely. He seized her and kissed her; she raised her lips to his, shyly at first, then with growing passion. They clung together in the field of waving flowers; she broke free first, and ran toward the stream which flowed down the slope, laughing, bending to toss her hands in the water.

Rafe thought in astonishment, *what has happened to us,* but the thought slid lightly over his mind and vanished. Camilla's slight body seemed to flicker, to go in and out of focus. She stripped off her climbing boots and thick socks, dabbling her feet in the water.

Rafe bent over her and pulled her down into the long grass.

In the camp on the lower heights, Heather Stuart woke slowly, feeling the hot sun through the orange silk of the tent. Marco Zabal still drowsed in his corner, his blanket drawn over his head; but as she looked at him he began to stir, and smiled at her.

"So you sleep too, still?"

"I suppose the others are out in the clearing," Heather said, stirring. "Judy said she wanted to test some of the nuts on the trees for edible carbohydrates—I notice her test kits aren't here. How are you feeling, Marco?"

"Better," he said, stretching. "I think maybe I get up for a minute today. Something in this air and sun, it does me good."

"It's lovely," she agreed. She too was conscious of some extra sense of well-being and euphoria in the scented air. *It must be the higher oxygen content.*

She stepped into the bright air, stretching like a cat in the sunshine.

A clear picture came into her mind, bright and intrusive and strangely exciting; Rafe, drawing Camilla into his arms. . . . "That's lovely," she said aloud, and breathed deeply, smelling the curious, somehow golden scent which seemed to fill the light warm wind.

"What's lovely? *You* are," said Ewen, coming around the tent and laughing. "Come on, let's walk in the forest—"

"Marco—"

"Marco's better. Do you realize that with all these people I've hardly spoken to you alone since before the crash?"

Hand in hand, they ran toward the trees; MacLeod, coming from the edge of the forest, his hands filled with ripe round clear-greenish fruits, held out a handful. His lips were dripping with their juice. "Here. They're marvelous—"

Laughing, Heather bit into the round smooth globe. It was bursting with sweet, fragrant juice; she ate it all, greedily, and reached for another. Ewen tried to pull it away.

"Heather, you're mad, they haven't even been tested yet—"

"I tested them," MacLeod laughed, "I ate half a dozen for breakfast and I feel wonderful! Say I'm psychic, if you like. They won't hurt you and they're chock full of every vitamin we know on Earth and a couple we don't! I *know*, I tell you!"

He caught Ewen's eye, and the young doctor, a curious awareness growing in him, said slowly, "Yes. Yes, you do know, of course they're good. Just as those mushrooms—" he pointed to a greyish fungus growing on the tree, "are wholesome and full of protein, but those—" he pointed to an exquisitely-colored golden nut, "are deadly, two bites will give you a hell of a bellyache and half a cup will kill you—how the hell do I know all this?" He rubbed his forehead, feeling the odd itch through it all, and took a fruit from Heather.

"Here, we'll all be crazy together then. Marvelous! Better than rations any day . . . where's Judy?"

"She's all right," MacLeod said, laughing. "I'm going off and look for some more fruits!"

Marco Zabal lay alone in the shelter-tent, eyes closed, half-dreaming through closed lids of the sun on the Basque hills of his childhood. Far away in the forest it seemed that he heard singing, singing which seemed to go on, and on, high and clear and sweet. He got to his feet, not stopping to draw any garment about him, disregarding the warning pounding of his heart. An incredible glow of well-being and beauty seemed to surge through him. The sunlight was brilliant on the sloping clearing, the trees seemed to hang darkly and protectively like a beckoning roof, the flowers seemed to sparkle and glitter with a brilliance that was like gold, orange, blue; colors he had never seen before danced and sparkled before his eyes.

Deep in the forest came the sound of singing, high, shrill, unbelievably sweet; the pipes of Pan, the lyre of

Orpheus, the call of the sirens. He felt his weakness fade; his youth restored.

Across the clearing he saw three of his companions, lying on the grass laughing, the girl kicking flowers into the air with her bare toes. He stood enraptured, watching her, entangled for a moment in the webs of her fantasy . . . *I am a woman made of flowers* . . . but the far-off singing lured him on; they beckoned him to join them, but he smiled, blew the girl a kiss, and bounded like a young man into the forest.

Far ahead he saw the gleam of white—a bird? A naked body?—he never knew how far he ran, hardly feeling the rapid pounding of his heart, wrapped in the glorious euphoria of freedom from pain, following the white gleam of the distant figure—or bird?—calling out in mingled rapture and anguish, "Wait, wait—"

The song shrilled and seemed to fill his whole head and heart. Gently, without pain, he fell into the long sweet-scented grass. The singing went on, and on, and he saw bending over him a fair face, long colorless hair waving around her eyes, a voice too sweet, too heart-wrenchingly sweet to be human, and hair turned to silver by the sun slanting through the trees, and he went happily, joyously down into darkness with the woman's face, sweet and mad, imprinted on his dying eyes.

Rafe ran through the forest, his heart pounding, slipping and falling on the steep path. He shouted, as he ran, "Camilla! Camilla!"

What had happened? One moment she was at peace in his arms—then pure terror had surged across her face and she had screamed and begun babbling something about faces on the heights, faces in the clouds, wide-open spaces waiting to fall on her and crush her, and the next moment she had wrenched away from him and dashed away between the trees, screaming wildly.

The trees seemed to waver and dip before his eyes, to form long black witch-claws to entangle him, tripping him up, throwing him full length into briars that raked along his arm and stung like fire. Lightning flashed with the color of the pain in his arm; he felt a wild and sudden terror as some unknown animal crashed a path in the forest, a stampede, hoofs, beating, beating, crushing him . . . he flung his arms around the bole of a tree and

53

clung to it, the pounding of his heart driving out all other thought. The tree's bark was soft and smooth, like the fur of some animal; he laid his hot face against it. Faces were watching him from the trees, faces, faces. . . .

"Camilla," he murmured, dazed, slipped to the ground and lay insensible.

On the heights, clouds gathered; fog began to rise. The wind died, and a thin fine rain began to fall, slowly turning to sleet; first on the heights, then in the valley. The flowers closed their bells; the bees and insects sought their holes in the tree-trunks and underbrush; and the pollen dropped, its work done, to the ground. . . .

Camilla woke, dazed, into dim darkness. She remembered nothing after she had run, screaming, panicked at the wideness as of interstellar space, nothing between her and the spreading stars . . . no. That had been delirium. Had it *all* been delirium? She explored slowly in the darkness, was rewarded by a gleam of light—a cave-mouth. She crept to the door of the cave and shivered with sudden icy cold. She was wearing only a thin cotton shirt and slacks, torn and disordered—no. Thank God, her parka was tied around her neck by its sleeves. Rafe had done it while they lay together by the bank of the stream.

Rafe. Where was he? Come to think of it, where was *she?* How much of the wild and disordered dreams were real and how much insane fantasy? Evidently she had caught some fever, some illness which lay in wait here. This horrible planet! This horrible place! How long had elapsed? Why was she alone here? Where were her scientific instruments, where her pack? Where—this was the burning question—where was Rafe?

She struggled into her parka and zipped it up, and felt the worst of the shivering subside, but she felt cold and hungry and nauseous, and her body ached and throbbed with a hundred scratches and bruises. Had Rafe left her here in the shelter of the cave while he went to fetch help? Had she been lying in fever and delirium for long? No, he would have left some message in case she recovered consciousness.

She looked through the falling snow, trying to figure out where she could possibly be. Above her, a dark slope rose. She must have dived into the cave in mad terror of the open spaces around her, seeking any darkness and shelter against the fear that lay on her. Perhaps MacAran was out in this wild weather looking for her, and they could wander for hours in the dark, missing one another by a few feet in the driving snow.

Logic bade her sit down and take stock of her situation. She was warmly clad now, and could shelter in the cave till daybreak. But suppose MacAran, too, was lost on the hillside? *Had it attacked them both, that sudden fear, that panic? And where had it come from, that joy, the abandon . . . No, that was for later, she couldn't think now about that.*

Where would MacAran seek her? The best thing was to climb up, toward the peak. Yes. They had left their packs there; and it was the one place from which they could orient themselves when the sun rose and the snow subsided. She would climb, and chance that logic would prompt MacAran to do the same. If not, and she found herself alone when dawn broke, she could make her way back to the camp where the others could help—or to the ship.

She climbed in the dark, driving snow, seeking each step for the way straight upward. After a time she began to guess that she was on the path they had made in their upward climb.

Yes. This is right. It was a sureness inside her, so that she began to move quickly in the dark, and after a time she saw, without surprise, a small bobbing light, making orange sparks against the snowflakes; and MacAran came straight toward her, and clasped her hands.

"How did you know where to look for me?" she asked.

"Hunch—or something," he said. In the small light of the handlamp she could just see the snow clinging to his eyebrows and lashes. "I just knew. Camilla—let's not waste breath on trying to figure it all out now. It's a long climb still to where we left our packs and equipment."

She said, twisting her lips in bitterness against the memory of how she had flung her pack from her, "Do you suppose they'll still be where we left them?"

MacAran's hand closed over hers. "Don't worry about it. Come," he added gently, "you need rest. We can talk about it some other time."

She relaxed, letting him guide her steps in the darkness. MacAran moved along at her side, exploring this new sureness and wondering from where it had come. Never for a moment had he doubted that he was moving directly toward Camilla in the darkness, he could *feel* her in front of him, but there was no way to say that without sounding quite mad.

They found the small shelter-tent set up in the lee of the rocks. Camilla crept inside gratefully, glad MacAran had spared her the struggle in the dark. MacAran felt confused; when had they set the tent up? Surely they had taken it down and stowed it in their packs before descending this morning? Had it been before or after they lay together by the stream-bank? The worry nagged at him but he dismissed it—we were both pretty freaked-out, we might have done *anything,* and hardly been conscious of it. He felt considerable relief at realizing that their packs were neatly piled inside—*God, we were lucky, might have lost all our calculations. . .*

"Shall I fix us something to eat before you sleep?"

She shook her head. "I couldn't eat. I feel as if I'd been dream-dusting! What *happened* to us, Rafe?"

"Search me." He felt unaccountably shy with her. "Did you eat anything in the forest—fruit, anything?"

"No. I remember wanting to, it looked so good, but at the last minute—I drank the water, though."

"Forget it. Water's water and Judy tested it, so that's out."

"Well, it must have been *something,*" she argued.

"I can't quarrel with that. But not tonight, please. We could hash it over for hours and not be any closer to an answer." He extinguished the light. "Try to sleep. We've already lost a day."

Into the darkness Camilla said, "Let's hope Heather was wrong about the blizzard, then."

MacAran didn't answer. He thought, did she say *blizzard,* or was it just *weather?* Could the freak weather have had anything to do with what happened? He had the uncanny sense, again, that he was near an answer and could not quite grasp it, but he was desperately tired, and it eluded him, and still groping, he slept.

Chapter
FIVE

They found Marco Zabal after a vain hour of searching and calling in the woods, laid out smooth and straight and already rigid beneath the greyish trunk of an unknown tree. The light snow had shrouded him in a pall a quarter of an inch thick, and at his side Judith Lovat knelt, so white and still beneath the drifting flakes that at first they thought in dismay that she had died too.

Then she stirred and looked up at them with dazed eyes and Heather knelt beside her, wrapping a blanket around her shoulders and trying to get her attention with soft words. She did not speak during all the time that MacLeod and Ewen were carrying Marco back to the tent, and Heather had to guide her steps as if she were drugged or in a trance.

As the small dismal procession wound through the falling snow Heather felt, or fantasied, that she could still feel their thoughts spinning in her own brain, Ewen's black despair . . . *what kind of doctor am I, lie fooling around on the grass while my patient runs out berserk and dies* . . . MacLeod's curious confusion entangled in her own fantasy, an old tale of the fairy folk she had heard in childhood, *the hero should never have woman or wife either of flesh and blood nor of the faery folk, and so they fashioned for him a woman made of flowers* . . . *I was the woman of flowers* . . .

Inside the tent Ewen sank down, staring straight ahead, and did not move. But Heather, desperately anxious at Judy's continued daze, went and shook him.

"Ewen! Marco's dead, there's nothing you can do for him, but Judy's alive; come and see if you can rouse her!"

Dragging, weary, *his thoughts look like a black cloud around him,* Heather thought, and shook herself. Ewen bent over Judith Lovat, checking her pulse, her heartbeat. He flashed a small light in her eyes, then said quietly, "Judy, did you lay out Marco's body the way we found it?"

"No," she whispered, "not I. It was the beautiful one, the beautiful one. I thought at first it was a woman, like a bird singing, and his eyes . . . his eyes . . ."

Ewen turned away in despair. "She's still delirious," he said shortly. "Fix her something to eat, Heather, and try to get it down her. We all need food—plenty of it; low blood sugar is half what's wrong with us now, I suspect."

MacLeod smiled a wry smile. "I got a contraband dose of Alpha happy-juice once," he said, "felt just about like that. What happened to us, anyhow, Ewen? You're the doctor, you tell us."

"As God is my witness, I don't know," Ewen said. "I thought at first it was the fruits, but we only began eating them *afterward*. And we all drank the water three days ago and no harm done. Anyway neither Judy nor Marco touched the fruit."

Heather put a bowl of hot soup into his hand, went and knelt by Judith, alternately spooning soup between her lips and trying to eat her own. MacLeod said, "I've no idea what happened first. It seemed like—I'm not sure; suddenly it was like a cold wind blowing through my bones, shaking me—shaking me *open* somehow. That was when I knew the fruits were good to eat and I ate one. . . ."

"Foolhardy," said Ewen, but MacLeod, still with that *openness*, knew that the young doctor was only cursing his own neglect. He said, "Why? The fruits *were* good, or we'd be sick now."

Heather said, hesitantly, "I can't help feeling it was something to do with the weather. Some difference."

"A psychedelic wind," jeered Ewen, "a ghostly wind that drove us all temporarily insane!"

"Stranger things have happened," Heather said, and artfully maneuvered another spoonful of soup into Judy's slack mouth. The older woman blinked dazedly and said, "Heather? How did I get here?"

"We brought you, love. You're all right now."

"Marco—I saw Marco—"

"He's dead," Ewen said gently, "he ran into the woods when we all went mad; I never saw him. He must have strained his heart—I'd warned him not even to sit up."

"It *was* his heart, then? You're sure?"

"As sure as I can be without autopsy, yes," Ewen

58

said. He swallowed the last of his soup. His head was clearing, but the guilt still lay on him; he knew he would never be wholly free of it. "Look, we've got to compare notes, while it's still fresh in our minds. There must be some one common factor, something we all did. Ate or drank—"

"Or breathed," Heather said. "It had to be something in the air, Ewen. Only the three of us ate the fruits. You didn't eat anything, did you, Judy?"

"Yes, some greyish stuff on the edge of a tree—"

"But we didn't touch that," Ewen said, "only MacLeod. We three ate the fruits, but neither Marco nor Judy did. MacLeod ate some of the grey fungus but none of us did. Judy was smelling the flowers and MacLeod was handling them, but neither Heather nor I did, until afterward. The three of us were lying in the grass—" he saw Heather's face turn pink, but went on steadily, "and both of us were making love to her, and all three of us were hallucinating. If Marco got up and ran into the woods I can only assume that he must have been hallucinating too. How did it begin with you, Judy?"

She only shook her head. "I don't know," she said. "I only know—the flowers were brighter, the sky seemed —seemed to break up like rainbows. Rainbows and prisms. Then I heard singing, it must have been birds, but I'm not sure. I went where the shadows were, and they were all purple, lilac-purple and blue. Then *he* came. . . ."

"Marco?"

She shook her head. "No. He was very tall, and had silver hair. . . ."

Ewen said pityingly, "Judy, you were hallucinating. I thought Heather was made out of flowers."

"The four moons—I could see them even though the sky was bright," Judy said. "He didn't say anything but I could hear him *thinking*."

MacLeod said, "We all seem to have had *that* delusion. If it's a delusion."

"It's sure to be," Ewen said. "We've found no trace of any other form of intelligent life here. Forget it, Judy," he added gently, "sleep. When we all get back to the ship—well, there will have to be some form of inquiry."

Dereliction, neglect of duty is the least it will be. Can I plead temporary insanity?

He watched Heather settle Judy down into her sleeping

bag. When the older woman finally slept he said wearily, "We ought to bury Marco. I hate to do it without an autopsy, but the only alternative is to carry him back to the ship."

MacLeod said, "We're going to look awfully damned foolish going back and claiming we all went mad at once." He did not look at Heather and Ewen as he added, rather sheepishly, "I feel like a ghastly fool—group sex never has been my kick—"

Heather said firmly, "We'll all have to forgive each other, and forget about it. It just happened, that's all. And for all we know it happened to them too—" she stopped, struck with a horrifying thought. "Imagine that sort of thing happening to *two hundred people*. . . ."

"It doesn't bear thinking about," MacLeod said with a shudder.

Ewen said that mass insanity was nothing new. "Whole villages. The dancing madness in the middle ages. And attacks of ergotism—from spoiled rye made into bread."

Heather said, "I don't think whatever it was got far enough down the mountain."

"Another of your hunches, I suppose," Ewen said, but not unkindly. "At this point I suspect we're all too close to it. Let's stop theorizing without facts and wait until we *have* some facts."

"Does this qualify as a fact?" Judy said, sitting up suddenly. They had all thought her asleep; she fumbled in the torn neck of her blouse and drew out something wrapped in leaves. "This—or these." She handed Ewen a small blue stone, like a star sapphire.

"Beautiful," he said slowly, "but you found it in the woods—"

"Right," she said. "I found this, too."

She stretched it out to him, and for a moment the others, crowding close, literally could not believe their eyes.

It was less than six inches long. The handle was made of something like shaped bone, delicate but quite without ornamentation. As for the rest, there was no question what it was.

It was a small flint knife.

Chapter
SIX

In the ten days the exploring party had been absent from the ship in the clearing, the clearing seemed to have grown. Two or three more small buildings had grown up around the ship; and at one edge of the clearing a fenced-off area had been plowed and a small sign proclaimed AGRICULTURAL TESTING AREA.

"That ought to do something for our food," MacLeod said, but Judith made no answer, and Ewen looked at her sharply. She had been curiously apathetic since That Day —that was how they all thought of it—and he was desperately worried about her. He wasn't a psychologist, but he knew that there was something gravely wrong. *Damn it, I did everything wrong. I let Marco die, I haven't been able to bring Judy back to reality.*

They came into the camp almost unnoticed, and for a moment MacAran felt a sharp stab of apprehension. Where was everybody? Had they all run amuck that day, had the madness overtaken all of them down here too? When he and Camilla had come down to the lower camp, to find Heather and Ewen and MacLeod still talking themselves hoarse in the attempt to find some explanation, it had been a bad moment. If madness lay on this planet, ready to claim them all, how could they survive? What worse things lay here waiting for them? Now, looking around the empty clearing, MacAran felt again the sharp stab of fear; then he saw a little group of people in Medic uniform coming out of the hospital tent, and further on, a crew going up into the ship. He relaxed; everything *looked* normal.

But then, so do we. . . .

"What's the first thing to do?" he asked. "Do we report straight to the Captain?"

"I should, at least," Camilla said. She looked thinner, almost haggard. MacAran wanted to take her hand and comfort her, although he was not sure for what. Since they had lain in each other's arms on the mountainside, he had felt a deep gnawing hunger for her, an almost fierce protectiveness; yet she turned away from him at every point, withdrawing into her old sharp self-sufficiency. MacAran felt hurt and resentful, and somehow lost. He dared not touch her, and it made him irritable.

"I expect he'll want to see all of us," he said. "We have to report Marco's death, and where we buried him. And we have a lot of information for him. Not to mention the flint knife."

"Yes. If the planet's inhabited that creates another problem," MacLeod said, but he did not elaborate.

Captain Leicester was with a crew inside the ship but an officer outside told the party that he had given orders that he was to be called the moment they returned, and sent for him. They waited in the small dome, none of them knowing what they were going to say.

Captain Leicester came into the dome. He looked somehow older, his face drawn with new lines. Camilla rose as he came in, but he motioned her to a seat again.

"Forget the protocol, Lieutenant," he said kindly, "you all look tired; was it a hard trip? I see Dr. Zabal is not with you."

"He's dead, sir," Ewen said quietly, "he died from the bites of poisonous insects. I'll make a complete report later."

"Make it to the Medic Chief," the Captain said, "I'm not qualified to understand anyway. You others can bring up your reports at the next meeting—tonight, I suppose. Mr. MacAran, did you manage to get the calculations you were hoping for?"

MacAran nodded. "Yes; as near as we can figure, the planet is somewhat larger than Earth, which means, with the lighter gravity, that its mass must be somewhat less. Sir, I can discuss all that later; just now I must ask you one question. Did anything unusual happen here while we were gone?"

The Captain's lined face ridged, displeased. "How do you mean, unusual? This whole planet is unusual, and nothing that happens here can be called routine."

Ewen said, "I mean anything like illness or mass insanity, sir."

Leicester frowned. "I can't imagine what you could be

talking about," he said. "No, no reports from Medic of any illness."

"What Dr. Ross means is that we all had an attack of something like delirium," MacAran told him. "It was the day after the second night without rain. It was widespread enough to hit Camilla—Lieutenant Del Rey—and myself, on the peaks, and to hit the other group almost six thousand feet lower down. We all behaved—well, irresponsibly, sir."

"Irresponsibly?" He scowled, his eyes fierce on them.

"Irresponsibly," Ewen met the Captain's eyes, his fists clenched. "Dr. Zabal was recovering; we ran off into the woods and left him alone so that he got up in delirium, ran off on his own and strained his heart—which is why he died. Judgment was imparied; we ate untested fruits and fungus. There were—various delusional processes."

Judith Lovat said firmly, "They were not all delusional."

Ewen looked at her and shook his head. "I don't think Dr. Lovat is in any state to judge, sir. We seem all to have had delusions about reading one another's thoughts, anyway."

The Captain drew a long, harried breath. "This will have to go to the Medics. No, we had nothing like that here. I suggest you all go and make your reports to the appropriate chiefs, or write them up to present at the meeting tonight. Lieutenant Del Rey, I want your report myself. I'll see the rest of you later."

"One more thing, sir," MacAran said. "This planet is inhabited." He drew out the flint knife from his pack, handed it over. But the Captain barely looked at it. He said, "Take it to Major Frazer; he's the staff anthropologist. Tell him I'll want a report tonight. Now if the rest of you will excuse us, please—"

MacAran felt the curious flatness of anticlimax as they left the Captain and Camilla together. While he hunted through the camp for anthropologist Frazer, he slowly identified his own feeling as jealousy. How could he compete with Captain Leicester? Oh, this was rubbish, the Captain was old enough to be Camilla's father. Did he honestly believe Camilla was in love with the Captain?

No. But she's emotionally all tied up with him and that's worse.

If he had been disappointed by the Captain's lack of

response to the flint knife, Major Frazer's response left nothing to be desired.

"I've been saying since we landed that this world was habitable," he said, turning the knife over in his hands, "and here's proof that it's inhabited—by something intelligent, at least."

"Humanoid?" MacAran asked, and Frazer shrugged. "How could we know that? There have been intelligent life-forms reported from three or four other planets; so far they have reported one simian, one feline, and three unclassifiable—xenobiology isn't my speciality. One artifact doesn't tell us anything—how many shapes are there that a knife could be designed in? But it fits a human hand well enough, although it's a little small."

Meals for crew and passengers were served in one large area, and when MacAran went for his noon meal he hoped to see Camilla; but she came in late and went directly to a group of other crew members. MacAran could not catch her eye and had the distinct feeling that she was avoiding him. While he was morosely eating his plateful of rations, Ewen came up to him.

"Rafe, they want us all at a Medical meeting if you have nothing else to do. They're trying to analyze what happened to us."

"Do you honestly think it will do any good, Ewen? We've all been talking it over—"

Ewen shrugged. "Mine is not to reason why," he said. "You're not under the authority of the Medic staff, of course, but still—"

MacAran asked, "Were they very rough on you about Zabal's death?"

"Not really. Both Heather and Judy testified that we were all out of contact. But they want your report, and everything you can tell them about Camilla."

MacAran shrugged and went along with him.

The Medic meeting was held at one end of the hospital tent, half empty now—the more seriously injured had died, the less so had been restored to duty. There were four qualified doctors, half a dozen nurses, and a few assorted scientific personnel to listen to the reports they made.

After listening to all of them in turn, the Chief Medical Officer, a dignified white-haired man named Di Asturien, said slowly, "It sounds like some form of airborne infection. Possibly a virus."

"But nothing like that turned up in our air samples," MacLeod argued, "and the effect was more like that of a drug."

"An airborne drug? It seems unlikely," Di Asturien said, "although the aphrodisiac effect seems to have been considerable also. Do I correctly assume that there was some sexual stimulation effect on all of you?"

Ewen said, "I already mentioned that, sir. It seemed to affect all three of us—Miss Stuart, Dr. MacLeod and myself. It had no such effect on Dr. Zabal to my knowledge, but he was in a moribund condition."

"Mr. MacAran?"

He felt for some strange reason embarrassed, but before Di Asturien's cool clinical eyes he said, "Yes, sir. You can check this with Lieutenant Del Rey if you like."

"Hm. I understand, Dr. Ross, that you and Miss Stuart are currently paired in any case, so perhaps we can discount that. But Mr. MacAran, you and the Lieutenant—"

"I'm interested in her," he said steadily, "but as far as I know she's completely indifferent to me. Even hostile. Except under the influence of—of whatever happened to us." He faced it, then. Camilla had not turned to him as a woman to a man she cared for. She had simply been affected by the virus, or drug, or whatever strange thing had sent them all mad. What to him had been love, to her had been madness—and now she resented it.

To his immense relief the Medic Chief did not pursue the subject. "Doctor Lovat?"

Judy did not look up. She said quietly, "I can't say. I can't remember. What I think I remember may very well be entirely delusion."

Di Asturien said, "I wish you would co-operate with us, Dr. Lovat."

"I'd rather not." Judy went on fingering something in her lap, and no persuasion could force her to say any more.

Di Asturien said, "In about a week, then, we'll have to test all three of you for possible pregnancy."

"How can that be necessary?" Heather asked. "I, at least, am taking regular anti shots. I'm not sure about

65

Camilla, but I suspect crew regulations require it for anyone between twenty and forty-five."

Di Asturien looked disturbed. "That's true," he said, "but there is something very peculiar which we discovered in a Medic meeting yesterday. Tell them, Nurse Raimondi."

Margaret Raimondi said, "I'm in charge of keeping records and issuing contraceptive and sanitary supplies for all women of menstrual age, both crew and passengers. You all know the drill; every two weeks, at the time of menstruation and halfway between, every woman reports for either a single shot of hormone or, in some cases, a patch strip to send small doses of hormones into the blood, which suppress ovulation. There are a total of one hundred and nineteen women surviving in the right age bracket, which means, with an average arbitrary cycle of thirty days, approximately four women would be reporting every day, either for menstrual supplies or for the appropriate shot or patch which is given four days after onset of menstruation. It's been ten days since the crash, which means about one-third of the women should have reported to me for one reason or the other. Say forty."

"And they haven't been," Dr. Di Asturien said. "How many women have reported since the crash?"

"Nine," said Nurse Raimondi grimly. *"Nine.* This means that two-thirds of the women involved have had their biological cycles disrupted on this planet—either by the change in gravity, or by some hormone disruption. And since the standard contraceptive we use is entirely keyed to the internal cycle, we have no way of telling whether it's effective or not."

MacAran didn't need to be told how serious this was. A wave of pregnancies could indeed be emotionally disruptive. Infants—or even young children—could not endure interstellar FTL drive; and since the universal acceptance of reliable contraceptives, and the population laws on overcrowded Earth, a wave of feeling had made abortion completely unthinkable. Unwanted children were simply never conceived. But would there be any alternative here?

Dr. Di Asturien said, "Of course, on new planets women are often sterile for a few months, largely because of the changes in air and gravity. But we can't count on it."

MacAran was thinking; *if Camilla is pregnant, will she*

66

hate me? The thought that a child of theirs might have to be destroyed was frightening. Ewen asked soberly, "What are we going to do, Doctor? We can't demand that two hundred adult men and women take a vow of chastity!"

"Obviously not. That would be worse for mental health than the other dangers," Di Asturien said, "but we must warn everyone that we're no longer sure about the effectiveness of our contraceptive program."

"I can see that. And as soon as possible."

Di Asturien said, "The Captain has called a mass meeting tonight—crew *and* colonists. Maybe I can announce it there." He made a wry face. "I'm not looking forward to it. It's going to be an awfully damned unpopular announcement. As if we didn't have enough troubles already!"

The mass meeting was held in the hospital tent, the only place big enough to hold the crew and passengers all at once. It had begun to cloud over by midafternoon and when the meeting was called, a thin fine cold rain was falling and distant lightning could be seen over the peaks of the hills. The members of the exploring party sat together at the front, in case they were called on for a report, but Camilla was not among them. She came in with Captain Leicester and the rest of the crew officers, and MacAran noticed that they had all put on formal uniform. Somehow that struck him as a bad sign. Why should they try to emphasize their solidarity and authority that way?

The electricians on the crew had put up a rostrum and rigged an elementary public address system, so that the Captain's voice, low and rather hoarse, could be heard throughout the big room.

"I have asked you all to come here tonight," he said, "instead of reporting only to your leaders, because in spite of every precaution, in a group this size rumors can get started, and can also get out of hand. First, I will give you what good news there is to give. To the best of our knowledge and belief, the air and water on this planet will support life indefinitely without damage to health, and the soil will probably grow Earth crops to supplement our food supply during the period of time while we are forced to remain here. Now I must give you the news which is not so good. The damage to the ship's drive units and computers is far more extensive than originally believed, and there is no possibility of immediate or rapid repairs. Although eventually it may be possible to become spaceborne, with our current personnel and materials, we cannot make repairs at all."

He paused, and a stir of voices, appalled, apprehensive, rose in the room. Captain Leicester raised his hand.

"I am not saying that we should lose hope," he said. "But in our current state we cannot make repairs. To get this ship off the surface of the planet is going to demand extensive changes in our present setup and will be a very long-range project demanding the total co-operation of every man and woman in this room."

Silence, and MacAran wondered what he meant by that. What exactly was the Captain saying? *Could* repairs be made or *couldn't* they?

"This may sound like a contradictory statement," the Captain went on. "We have not the material to make repairs. However, we *do* have, among all of us, the *knowledge* to make repairs; and we have an unexplored planet at our disposal, where we can certainly find the raw materials and *build* the material to make repairs."

MacAran frowned, wondering exactly how that was meant. Captain Leicester proceeded to explain.

"Many of you people bound for the colonies have skills which will be useful there but which are of no use to us here," he said. "Within a day or two we will set up a personnel department to inventory all known skills. Some of you who have registered as farmers or artisans will be placed under the direction of our scientists or engineers to be trained. I demand a total push."

At the back of the room, Moray rose. He said, "May I ask a question, Captain?"

"You may."

"Are you saying that the two hundred of us in this room can, within five or ten years, develop a technological culture capable of building—or rebuilding—a starship? That we can discover the metals, mine them, refine them, machine them, and build the necessary machinery?"

The Captain said quietly, "With the full co-operation of every person here, this can be done. I estimate that it will take between three and five years."

Moray said flatly, "You're insane. You're asking us to evolve a whole technology!"

"What man has done, man can do again," Captain

68

Leicester said imperturbably. "After all, Mr. Moray, I remind you that we have no alternative."

"The hell we don't!"

"You are out of order," the Captain said sternly. "Please take your seat."

"No, damn it! If you really believe all this can be done," Moray said, "I can only assume that you're stark raving mad. Or that the mind of an engineer or spaceman works so differently from any sane man's that there's no way to communicate. You say this will take three to five years. May I respectfully remind you that we have about a year to eighteen months' supply of food and medical supplies? May I also remind you that even now —moving toward summer—the climate is harsh and rigorous and our shelters are insufficient? The winter on this world, with its exaggerated tilt on the axis, is likely to be more brutal than anything any Earthman has ever experienced."

"Doesn't that prove the necessity of getting off this world as soon as possible?"

"No, it proves the need of finding reliable sources of food and shelter," Moray said. *"That's* where we need our total push! Forget your ship, Captain. It isn't going anywhere. Come to your senses. We're colonists, not scientists. We have everything we need to survive here—to settle down here. But we can't do it if half our energies are devoted to some senseless plan of diverting all our resources to repair a hopelessly crashed ship!"

There was a small uproar in the hall, a flood of cries, questions, outrage. The Captain repeatedly called for order, and finally the cries died down to dull mutterings. Moray demanded, "I call for a vote," and the uproar rose again.

The Captain said, "I refuse to consider your proposal, Mr. Moray. The matter will not come to a vote. May I remind you that I am currently in supreme command of this ship? Must I order your arrest?"

"Arrest, hell," Moray said scornfully. "You're not in space now, Captain. You're not on the bridge of your ship. You have no authority over any of us, Captain— except maybe your own crew, if they want to obey you."

Leicester stood on the rostrum, as white as his shirt, his eyes gleaming with fury. He said, "I remind all of you that MacAran's party, sent out to explore, has discovered traces of intelligent life on this planet. Earth Expeditionary has a standard policy of not placing colonies on inhabited planets. If we settle here we are likely to bring cultural shock to the stone age culture."

Another uproar. Moray shouted angrily, "Do you think your attempts to evolve a technology here for your repairs wouldn't do that? In God's name, sir, we have everything we need to establish a colony here. If we divert all our resources to your insane effort to repair the ship, it's doubtful if we can even survive!"

Captain Leicester made a distinct effort to master himself, but his fury was obvious. He said harshly, "You are suggesting that we abandon the effort—and relapse into barbarism?"

Moray was suddenly very grave. He came forward to the rostrum and stood beside the Captain. His voice was level and calm.

"I hope not, Captain. It is man's mind that makes him a barbarian, not his technology. We may have to do without top-level technology, at least for a few generations, but that doesn't mean we can't establish a good world here for ourselves and our children, a civilized world. There have been civilizations which have existed for centuries almost without technology. The illusion that man's culture is only the history of his technostructures is propaganda from the engineers, sir. It has no basis in sociology—or in philosophy."

The Captain said harshly, "I'm not interested in your social theories, Mr. Moray."

Doctor Di Asturien rose. He said, "Captain, one thing must be taken into account. We made a most disquieting discovery today—"

At that moment a violent clap of thunder rocked the hospital tent. The hastily rigged lights went out. And from the door one of the security men shouted:

"Captain! Captain! The woods are on fire!"

Chapter
SEVEN

Everyone kept their heads; Captain Leicester bellowed from the platform, "Get some lights in here; security, get some lights!" One of the young men on the Medic staff found a handlamp for the Captain and one of the bridge officers shouted, "Everyone! Stay in place and wait for orders, there is no danger here! Get those lights rigged as fast as you can!"

MacAran was near enough to the door to see the distant rising glare against the darkness. In a few minutes lamps were being distributed, and Moray, from the platform, said urgently, "Captain, we have tree-felling and earth-moving equipment. Let me order a detail to work on firebreaks around the encampment."

"Right, Mr. Moray. Get with it," Leicester said harshly. "All bridge officers, gather here; get to the ship and secure any flammable or explosive material." He hurried away toward the back of the tent. Moray ordered all able-bodied men to the clearing, and requisitioned all available handlamps not in use on the bridge. "Form up in the same squads you did for gravedigging detail," he ordered. MacAran found himself in a crew with Father Valentine and eight strangers, felling trees in a ten-foot swath around the clearing. The fire was still a distant roar on a slope miles away, a red glare against the sky, but the air smelled of smoke, with a strange acrid undertone.

Someone said at MacAran's elbow, "How can the woods catch fire after all this rain?"

He brought back memory of something Marco Zabal had said that first night. "The trees are heavily resined—practically tinder. Some few of them may even burn when they're wet—we built a campfire of green wood. I suppose lightning can set off a fire at almost any time." We were lucky, he thought, we camped out in the center of the woods and never thought of fire, or of firebreaks. "I

71

suspect we'll need a permanent firebreak around any encampment or work area."

Father Valentine said, "You sound as if you thought we were going to be here a long time."

MacAran bent to his saw. He said, not looking up, "No matter whose side you're on—the Captain's or Moray's—it looks as if we'd be here for years." He was too weary, and too unsure of anything at this moment, to decide for himself if he had any real preference and in any case he was sure no one would consult him about his choice, but down deep he knew that if they ever left this world again he would regret it.

Father Valentine touched his shoulder. "I think the Lieutenant is looking for you."

He straightened to see Camilla Del Rey walking toward him. She looked worn and haggard, her hair uncombed and her uniform dirty. He wanted to take her in his arms but instead he stood and watched her attempt not to meet his eyes as she said, "Rafe, the Captain wants to talk with you. You know the terrain better than anyone else. Do you think it could be fought or contained?"

"Not in the dark—and not without heavy equipment," MacAran said, but he accompanied her back toward the Captain's field quarters. He had to admire the efficiency with which the firebreak operation had been set up, the small amount of ship's firefighting equipment moved to the hospital. *The Captain had sense enough to use Moray here. They're really two of a kind—if they could only work together for the same objectives. But just now they're the irresistible force and the immovable object.*

The fine rain was changing to heavy sleet as they came into the dome. The small dark crowded dome was dimly lit by a single handlamp, and the battery seemed to be already failing.

Moray was saying: "—our power sources are already giving way. Before we can do anything else, sir, in your plan *or* mine, some sources of light and heat have to be found. We have wind-power and solar-power equipment in the colonizing materials, although I somehow doubt if this sun has enough light and radiation for much solar power. MacAran—" he turned, "I take it there are mountain streams? Any big enough for damming?"

"Not that we saw in the few days we were in the mountains," MacAran said, "but there's plenty of wind."

"That will do for a temporary makeshift," Captain Leicester said. "MacAran, do you know exactly where the fire is located?"

"Far enough to be no immediate danger to us," MacAran said, "although we're going to need firebreaks from now on, anywhere we go. But this fire's no danger, I think. The rain's turning to snow and I think that will smother it out."

"If it can burn in the rain—"

"Snow's wetter and heavier," MacAran said, and was interrupted by what sounded like a volley of gunfire. "What's that?"

Moray said, "Game stampede—probably getting away from the fire. Your officers are shooting food. Captain, once again, I suggest conservation of ammunition for absolute emergencies. Even on Earth, game has been hunted recreationally with bow and arrow. There are prototypes in the recreation department, and we'll need them for enlarging the food supply."

"Full of ideas, aren't you," Leicester grunted, and Moray said, tight-mouthed, "Captain, running a spaceship is your business. Setting up a viable society with the most economical use of resources is *mine*."

For a moment the two men stared at one another in the failing light, the others in the dome forgotten. Camilla had edged around behind the Captain and it seemed to MacAran that she was supporting him mentally as well as backing him up physically. Outside there were all the noises of the camp, and behind it all the small hiss of snow striking the dome. Then a gust of high wind struck it and a blast of cold air came in through the flapping doorway; Camilla ran to shut it, struggling against the wild blast, and was flung back. The door swung wildly, came loose from the makeshift hinges and knocked the girl off her feet; MacAran ran to help her up. Captain Leicester swore softly and began to shout for one of his aides.

Moray raised a hand. He said quietly, "We need stronger and more permanent shelters, Captain. These were built to last six weeks. May I order them built to last for a few years, then?"

Captain Leicester was silent, and with that new and exaggerated sensitivity it almost seemed to MacAran that he could hear what the Captain was thinking. Was this an entering wedge? Could he use Moray's undoubted talents without giving him too much power over the colonists, and diminishing his own? When he spoke his voice was bitter; but he gave way gracefully.

"You know survival, Mr. Moray. I'm a scientist—and a spaceman. I'll put you in charge of the camp, on a temporary basis. Get your priorities in order and requisition what you need." He strode to the door and stood there looking out at the whirling snow. "No fire can live in that. Call in the men and feed them before they go back to making firebreaks. You're in charge, Moray—for the time being." His back was straight and indomitable, but he sounded tired. Moray bowed slightly. There was no hint of subservience in it.

"Don't think I'm giving way," Leicester warned. "That ship is going to be repaired."

Moray shrugged a little. "Maybe so. But it can't be repaired unless we survive long enough to do it. For now, that's all I'm concerned about."

He turned to Camilla and MacAran, ignoring the Captain.

"MacAran, your party knows at least some of the terrain. I want a local survey made of all resources, including food—Dr. Lovat can handle that. Lieutenant Del Rey, you're a navigator; you have access to instruments. Can you arrange to make some sort of climate survey which we might manage to use for weather prediction?" He broke off. "The middle of the night isn't the time for this. We'll get moving tomorrow." He moved to the door and, finding his way blocked by Captain Leicester standing and staring into the whirling snowflakes, tried to move past him a time or two, finally touched him on the shoulder. The Captain started and moved aside. Moray said, "The first thing to do is to get those poor devils in out of the storm. Will you give orders, Captain, or shall I?"

Captain Leicester met his eyes levelly and with taut hostility. "It doesn't matter," he said quietly, "I'm not concerned with which of us gives the orders, and God help you, if *you're* just looking for the power to give them. Camilla, go and tell Major Layton to secure from firefighting operations and make sure that everyone who was on the firebreak line gets hot food before he turns in." The girl pulled her hood over her head and hurried off through the snow.

"You may have your talents, Moray," he said, "and as far as I'm concerned you're welcome to use mine. But there's an old saying in the Space Service. Anyone who intrigues for power, deserves to get it!"

He strode out of the dome, leaving the wind to blow through it, and MacAran, watching Moray, felt that somehow, obscurely, the Captain had come off best.

Chapter
EIGHT

The days were lengthening, but even so there seemed never to be enough light or enough time for the work which had to be done in the settlement. Three days after the fire, extensive firebreaks thirty feet wide had been constructed around the encampment, and firefighting squads had been organized for emergency outbreaks. It was about that time that MacAran went off, with a party of the colonists, to make Moray's survey. The only members of the previous party to accompany him were Judith Lovat and MacLeod. Judy was still quiet and contained, almost unspeaking; MacAran was worried about her, but she did her work efficiently and seemed to have an almost psychic awareness of where to find the sort of thing they were looking for.

For the most part, this woodland exploration trip was uneventful. They laid out trails for possible roadways toward the valley where they had first seen herds of game, assessed the amount of fire damage—which was not really very great—mapped the local streams and rivers, and MacAran collected rock samples from the local heights to assess their potential ore contents.

Only one major event broke the rather pleasant monotony of the trip. One evening toward sunset they were blazing trail through an unusually thick level of forest when MacLeod, slightly ahead of the main party, stopped short, turned back, laying a finger on his lips to enjoin silence, and beckoned to MacAran.

MacAran came forward, Judy tiptoeing at his side. She looked oddly excited.

MacLeod pointed upward through the thick trees. Two huge trunks rose dizzyingly high, without auxiliary branches for at least sixty feet; and spanning them, swung a bridge. There was nothing else to call it; a bridge of what looked like woven wickerwood, elaborately constructed with handrails.

MacLeod said in a whisper, "There are the proofs of your aborigines. Can they be arboreal? Is that why we haven't seen them?"

Judy said sharply, "Hush!" In the distance there was a small, shrill, chattering sound; then, above them on the bridge, a creature appeared.

They all got a good look at it in that moment; about five feet tall, either pale-skinned or covered with pale fur, gripping the bridge rail with undoubted hands—none of them had presence of mind to count the fingers—a flat but oddly humanoid face, with a flat nose and red eyes. For nearly ten seconds it clung to the bridge and looked down at them, seeming nearly as startled as they were themselves; then, with a shrill birdlike cry it rushed across the bridge, swung up into the trees and vanished.

MacAran let out a long sigh. So this world was inhabited, not free and open for mankind. MacLeod asked quietly, "Judy, were these the people you saw that day? The one you called *the beautiful one?*"

Judy's face took on the strange stubbornness which any mention of that day could bring on. "No," she said, quietly but very positively. "These are the little brothers, the small ones who are not wise."

And nothing could move her from that, and very quickly they gave over questioning her. But MacLeod and Major Fraser were in seventh heaven.

"Arboreal humanoids. Nocturnal, to judge by their eyes, probably simian, although more like tarsiers than apes. Obviously sapient—they're tool-users and makers of artifacts. *Homo arborens.* Men living in trees," MacLeod said.

MacAran said hesitatingly, "If we have to stay here—how can two sapient species survive on one planet?

76

Doesn't that invariably mean a fatal war for dominance?"

Fraser said, "God willing, no. After all, there were four sapient species on Earth for a long time. Mankind—and dolphins, whales, and probably elephants too. We just happened to be the only *technological* species. They're tree-dwelling; we're ground-dwelling. No conflict, as far as I can see—anyway no *necessary* conflict."

MacAran wasn't so sure, but kept his qualms to himself.

Peaceful as their trip was, there were unexpected dangers. In the valley with the game, which they named for convenience the Plains of Zabal, the game was stalked by great catlike predators and only nighttime fires kept them away. And on the heights MacAran caught his first sight of the birds with the banshee voices; great wingless birds with vicious claws, moving at such speeds that only a last desperate recourse to the laser beam they carried for emergencies kept Dr. Fraser from being disemboweled by a terrible stroke; MacLeod, dissecting the dead bird, discovered that it was completely blind. "Does it get at its prey by hearing? Or something else?"

"I suspect it senses body warmth," MacAran said, "they seem only to live in the snows." They christened the dreadful birds *banshees*, and avoided the passes except in broad daylight after that. They also found mounds of the scorpion-like ants whose bites had killed Dr. Zabal, and debated poisoning them; MacLeod was against it, on the grounds that these ants might form some important part of an ecological chain which could not be disturbed. They finally agreed to exterminate only the mounds within three square miles of the ship, and warn everyone about the dangers of their bite. It was an interim measure, but then everything they did on this planet was an interim measure.

"If we leave the damn place," Dr. Fraser said harshly, "we'll have to leave it pretty much the way we found it."

When they returned to the encampment, after a three week survey, they found that two permanent buildings of wood and stone had already been erected; a common recreation hall and refectory, and a building for use as a laboratory. It was the last time MacAran measured anything by weeks; they still did not know the length of the planet's year, but they had for the sake of convenience

77

and the assignment of duties and work shifts set up an arbitrary ten-day cycle, with one day in every ten a general holiday. Large gardens had been laid out and seeds were already sprouting, and a careful harvesting was being made of a few tested fruits from the woods.

A small wind generator had been rigged, but power was strictly rationed, and candles made from resin from the trees were being issued for night use. The temporary domes still housed most of the personnel except those who were located in the hospital; MacAran shared his with a dozen other single men.

The day after his return Ewen Ross summoned both him and Judy to the hospital. "You missed Dr. Di Asturien's announcement," he said. "In brief, our hormone contraceptives are worthless—no pregnancies so far except one very doubtful early miscarriage, but we've been relying on hormones so long that no one knows much about the prehistoric kind any more. We don't have pregnancy-testing equipment, either, since nobody needs it on a spaceship. Which means if we *do* get any pregnancies they may be too far advanced for safe abortions before they're even diagnosed!"

MacAran smiled wryly. "You can save your breath where I'm concerned," he said, "the only girl I'm currently interested in doesn't know I'm alive—or at least wishes I weren't." He had not even seen Camilla since his return.

Ewen said, "Judy, what about you? I looked up your Medic record; you're at the age where contraception is voluntary instead of mandatory—"

She smiled faintly. "Because at my age I'm not likely to be taken unawares by emotion. I've not been sexually active on this voyage—there's no one I've been interested in, so I've not bothered with the shots."

"Well, check with Margaret Raimondi anyhow—she's giving out emergency information just in case. Sex is voluntary, Judy, but information is mandatory. You can choose to abstain—but you ought to be free to choose not to, so run along to Margaret and pick up the information."

She began to laugh and it struck MacAran that he had not seen Judith Lovat laugh since the day of the strange madness that had attacked them all. But the laughing seemed to have a hysterical note which made him uneasy,

78

and he was relieved when she said at last, "Oh, very well. What harm can it do?" and went. Ewen looked after her with disquiet, too.

"I'm not happy about her. She seems to have been the only one permanently affected by whatever it was that hit us, but we haven't psychiatrists to spare and anyhow she is able to do her work—which is a legal definition of sanity in any terms. Still, I hope she snaps out of it. Was she all right on the trip?"

MacAran nodded. He said thoughtfully, "Perhaps she had some experience she hasn't told us about. She certainly seems at home here. Something like what you told me about MacLeod knowing the fruits were good to eat. Could an emotional shock develop latent psi powers?"

Ewen shook his head. "God only knows, and we're too busy to check it out. Anyhow, how would you check out anything like that? As long as she's normal enough to do her assigned work I can't interfere with her."

After leaving the hospital, MacAran walked through the encampment. Everything looked peaceful, from the small shop where farm tools were being constructed, to the ship area where machinery was being removed and stored. He found Camilla in the dome which had been wind-damaged the night of the fire; it had been repaired and reinforced, and the computer controls set up inside. She looked at him with what seemed open hostility.

"What do you want? Has Moray sent you here to order me to transform this into a weather station or some such thing?"

"No, but it sounds like a good idea," MacAran said. "Another blizzard like the one that hit us the night of the fire, could wreck us if we weren't warned."

She came and looked up at him. Her arms were straight down at her sides, clenched into fists, and her face taut with anger. She said, "I think you must all be quite insane. I don't expect anything more of the colonists —they're just civilians and all they care about is getting their precious colony set up. But you, Rafe! You've had a scientist's training, you ought to see what it *means!* All we *have* is the hope of repairing the ship—if we waste our resources on anything else, the chances get smaller and smaller!" She sounded frantic. "And we'll be here forever!"

MacAran said slowly, "Remember, Camilla, I was one

79

of the colonists, too. I left Earth to join the Coronis colony—"

"But that's a regular colony, with everything set up to make it—to make it part of civilization," Camilla said. "I can understand *that*. Your skills, your education, they'd be *worth* something!"

MacAran reached out and took her shoulders in his hands. "Camilla—" he said, and put all his yearning into the sound of her name. She didn't actually respond, but she was quiet between his hands, looking up at him. Her face was drawn and miserable.

"Camilla, will you listen to me a minute? I'm with the Captain all the way, as far as acts go. I'm willing to do anything needful to make sure the ship gets off the ground. But I'm keeping in mind that it may not, after all, be possible, and I want to make sure we can survive if it isn't."

"Survive for what?" Camilla said, almost frantic. "To revert to savagery, survive as farmers, barbarians, with nothing that makes life worth living? We'd do better to die in a last effort!"

"I don't know why you say that, my love. After all, the first humans started with less than we have. Their world, maybe, had a little better climate, but then we have ten or twelve thousand years of human know-how. A group of people that Captain Leicester thinks capable of repairing a starship, ought to have enough know-how to build a pretty good life for themselves and their children—and all the generations after that." He tried to draw her into his arms, but she wrenched away, white and furious.

"I'd rather *die*," she said harshly, "any civilized human being would! You're worse than the New Hebrides group out there—Moray's people—that damnfool back-to-nature crew, playing right into his hands—"

"I don't know anything about them—Camilla, my darling, please don't be angry with me. I'm only trying to look at both sides—"

"But there *is* only one side," she flung at him, angry and implacable, "and if you don't see it that way then you aren't even worth talking with! I'm ashamed—I'm ashamed of myself that I ever let myself think you might be different!" Tears were running down her face, and she angrily flung off his hands. "Get out and stay out! Get out, damn you!"

MacAran had the temper usually associated with his hair. He dropped his hands as if he had been burned, and spun on his heel. "It will be a positive pleasure," he said between his teeth, and strode out of the dome, slamming the reinforced door until it rattled on its hinges. Behind him Camilla collapsed on a bench, her face in her hands, and cried herself sick, weeping frantically until a wave of violent nausea racked her, forcing her to stagger away toward the women's latrine area. At last she crept away, her head pounding, her face flushed and sore, aching in every nerve.

As she returned to the computer dome, a memory struck her. This had happened three times now—in a surge of violent fear and rejection, her hands went up to her mouth, and she bit at her knuckles.

"Oh, no," she whispered, "Oh, no, no . . ." and her voice trailed off in whispered pleas and imprecations. Her grey eyes were wild with terror.

MacAran had gone into the combined recreation area-refectory, which had quickly become a center for the huge and disorganized community, when he noticed on an improvised bulletin board a notice about a meeting of the New Hebrides Commune. He had seen this before—the colonists accepted by Earth Expeditionary had consisted not only of individuals like himself and Jenny, but of small groups or communes, extended families, even two or three business companies wishing to extend their trade or open branch offices. They were all carefully screened to determine how they would fit into the balanced development of the colony, but apart from that they were a most heterogeneous crew. He suspected that the New Hebrides Commune was one of the many small neo-rural communes who had drawn away from the mainstream society on latter-day Earth, resenting its industrialization and regimentation. Many such communities had gone out to the star colonies; everyone agreed that while misfits on Earth, they made excellent colonists. He had never paid the slightest attention to them before; but after Camilla's words he was curious. He wondered if their meeting was open to outsiders?

He vaguely remembered that this group had occasionally reserved one of the ship's recreation areas for their own meetings, they seemed to have a strongly knit community life. Well, at worst they could ask him to leave.

He found them in the empty, between-meal refectory area. Most of them were sitting in a circle and playing musical instruments; one of them, a tall youth with long braided hair, raised his head and said, "Members only, friend," but another, a girl with red hair hanging loose to her waist, said, "No, Alastair. It's MacAran, and he was on the exploring team, he knows a lot of the answers we need. Come in, man, make yourself welcome."

Alastair laughed. "Right you are, Fiona, and with a name like MacAran he should be an honorary member anyway."

MacAran came in. To his faint surprise he saw, somewhere in the circle, the round, pudgy, ginger-haired little figure of Lewis MacLeod. He said, "I didn't meet any of you on the ship, I'm afraid I don't know what you people are supposed to stand for."

Alastair said quietly, "We're neo-ruralists, of course; world-builders. Some members of the Establishment call us anti-technocrats, but we're not the destroyers. We're simply looking for an honorable alternative for the society of Earth, and we're usually just as welcome in the colonies as they are glad to have us away from Earth. So—tell us, MacAran. What's the story here? How soon can we get out to make our own settlement?"

MacAran said, "You know as much as I do. The climate is pretty brutal, you know; if it's like this in summer, it's going to be a lot rougher in winter."

Fiona laughed. She said, "Most of us grew up in the Hebrides or even the Orkneys. They have about the worst climate on Earth. Cold doesn't scare us, MacAran. But we want to be established in community life, so we can set up our own ways and customs, before the winter sets in."

MacAran said slowly, "I'm not sure Captain Leicester will let anyone leave the encampment. The priority is still on repairing the ship, and I think he regards all of us as a single community. If we begin to break up—"

"Come *off* it," Alastair said, "none of us are scientists. We can't spend five years working on a starship; it's against our entire philosophy!"

"Survival—"

"—survival." MacAran understood only a little of the

82

Gaelic of his forefathers, but he realized Alastair was being indecent. "Survival, to us, means setting up a colony here as fast as possible. We signed on to go to Coronis. Captain Leicester made a mistake and set us down here, but it's all the same to us. For our purposes, this is even better."

MacAran raised his eyebrows at MacLeod. He said, "I didn't know you belonged to this group."

"I didn't," MacLeod said, "I'm a fringe member, but I agree with them—and I want to stay here."

"I thought they didn't approve of scientists."

The girl Fiona said, "Only in their place. When they use their knowledge to serve and help mankind—not to manipulate it, or to destroy its spiritual strength. We're happy to have Dr. MacLeod—Lewis, we don't use titles—as one of us, with his knowledge of zoology."

MacAran said, in amazement, "Are you intending to mutiny against Captain Leicester?"

"Mutiny? We're not his crew or his subjects, man," said a strange boy, "we just intend to live the way we would have made for ourselves on the new world. We can't wait three years until he gives up this wild idea of rebuilding his ship. By that time we could have a functional community."

"And if he does repair the ship, and goes on to Coronis? Will you stay here?"

"This is our world," the girl Fiona said, coming to Alastair's side. Her eyes were gentle but implacable. "Our children will be born here."

MacAran said, in shock, "Are you trying to tell me—"

Alastair said, "We don't know, but some of our women may already be pregnant. It is our sign of commitment to this world, our sign of rejection of Earth and the world Captain Leicester wants to force on us. And you can tell him so."

As MacAran left them, the musical instruments began again, and the mournful sound of a girl's voice, in the eternal melancholy of an old song of the Isles; a lament for the dead, out of a past more torn and shattered with wars and exiles than any other people of Earth:

> Snow-white seagull, say,
> Tell me, pray,
> Where our fair young lads are resting.

83

Wave on wave they lie,
Breath nor sigh,
From their cold lips coming;
Sea-wrack their shroud,
Harp and dirge the sea's sad crooning.

The song tightened MacAran's throat, and against his will tears came to his eyes. *They lament,* he thought, *but they know life goes on. The Scots have been exiles for centuries, for millennia. This is just another exile, a little further than most, but they will sing the old songs under the new stars and find new mountains and new seas. . . .*

Going out of the hall he drew up his hood—by now it would be beginning to rain. But it wasn't.

Chapter
NINE

MacAran had already seen what a couple of rainless and snowless nights could do on this planet. The garden areas blossomed with vegetation, and flowers, mostly the small orange ones, covered the ground everywhere. The four moons came out in their glory from before sunset until well after sunrise, turning the sky into a flood of lilac brilliance.

The woods were dry, and they began to worry about keeping a firewatch. Within a few miles of the encampment, Moray got the idea of rigging lightning-rods to each of the hilltops, each anchored to an enormously tall tree. It might not prevent fire in the event of a serious storm, but might lessen the dangers somewhat.

And above them on the heights, the great bell-shaped golden flowers opened wide, their sweet-scented pollen drifting in the upper slopes. It had not reached the valleys.

Not yet. . . .

After a week of snowless evenings, moonlit nights and warm days—warm by the standards of this planet, which would have made Norway seem like a summer resort—MacAran went to ask Moray's assent to another trip into the foothills. He felt he should take advantage of the rare seasonable weather to collect further geological specimens, and perhaps to locate caves which might serve as emergency shelter during later exploration. Moray had taken a small room at the corner of the Recreation building for an office, and while MacAran waited outside, Heather Stuart came into the building.

"What do you think of this weather?" he asked her, the old habit from Earth asserting itself. *When in doubt talk about the weather. Well, there's plenty of weather on this planet to talk about, and it's all so bad.*

"I don't like it," Heather said seriously, "I haven't forgotten what happened on the mountain when we had a few clear days."

You too? MacAran thought, but he demurred. "How could the weather be responsible, Heather?"

"Airborne virus. Airborne pollen. Dust-borne chemicals. I'm a microbiologist, Rafe, you'd be surprised what can be in a few cubic inches of air or water or soil. In the debriefing session Camilla said the last thing she remembered before freaking out was smelling the flowers, and I remember that the air was full of their scent." She smiled weakly. "Of course what I remember may not be any kind of evidence and I hope to God that I don't find out by trial and error again. I've just found out for certain that I'm not pregnant, and I never want to go through *that* again. When I think of the way women must have had to live before the really safe contraceptives were invented, from month to month never *knowing*. . . ." She shuddered. "Rafe, is Camilla sure yet? She won't talk to me about it any more."

"I don't know," MacAran said sombrely, "she won't talk to me at all."

Heather's fair mobile face registered dismay. "Oh, I'm so sorry, Rafe! I was so happy about you two, Ewen and I both hoped—oh, here, I think maybe Moray's ready to see you." The door had opened and the big redhead Alastair bumped into them as he came barging out; he turned and half shouted, "The answer is still *no,* Moray! We're pulling out—all of us, our whole Community! Now, tonight!"

Moray followed him to the door. He said, "Selfish crew,

85

aren't you? You talk about community, and it turns out that you mean only your own little group—not the larger community of mankind on this planet. Did it ever occur to you that all of us, the whole two-hundred-odd of us, are perforce a commune? We *are* humanity, we *are* society. Where's that big sense of responsibility toward your fellow man, laddie?"

Alastair bent his head. He muttered, "The rest of you don't stand for what we stand for."

"We all stand for common good and survival," Moray said quietly. "The Captain will come around. Give me a chance to talk to the others, at least."

"I was appointed to speak for them—"

"Alastair," said Moray gravely, "you're violating your own standards, you know. If you're a true philosophical anarchist, you have to give them an opportunity to hear what I have to say."

"You're just trying to manipulate us all—"

"Are you afraid of what I'll say to them? Are you afraid they won't stick to what *you* want?"

Alastair, maneuvered into a corner, burst out, "Oh, talk to them and be damned to you, then! Much good may it do you!"

Moray followed them out, saying to MacAran as he passed, "Whatever it is, it'll have to keep, lad. I have to talk these young lunatics into trying to see us all as one big family—not just their little family!"

Out in the open space, the thirty members or so of the New Hebrides community were gathered. MacAran noticed that they had put aside the ship-issued surface uniform and were wearing civilian clothing and carrying backpacks. Moray went forward and began to harangue them. From where he stood at the door of the Recreation Hall MacAran could not hear his words, but there was a lot of shouting and argument. MacAran stood watching the small swirls and eddies of dust blow up across the plowed ground, the backlog of wind in the trees at the edge of the clearing like a sea-noise that never quieted. It seemed to him that there was a song in the wind. He looked down at Heather beside him, and her face seemed to gleam and glow in the dark sunlight, almost a visible song.

She said hoarsely, "Music—music on the wind. . . ."

MacAran muttered, "In God's name what are they doing out there? Holding a *dance?*"

He moved away from Heather, as a group of the uniformed Security guards came across from the ship. One of them faced Alastair and Moray and started to speak; MacAran, moving into range, heard "—put down your packs. I have the Captain's orders to take you all into custody, for desertion in the face of an emergency."

"Your Captain hasn't any power over us, emergency or otherwise, fuzz-face," the big redhead yelled, and one of the girls scooped up a handful of dirt and flung it, evoking screams of riotous laughter from the others.

Moray said urgently to the Security men, "No! There is no need for this! Let me handle them!"

The officer hit by the thrown dirt unslung his gun. MacAran, gripped by a surge of all too familiar fear, muttered, "That's torn it," and ran forward just as the young men and women of the communes threw down their rucksacks and charged, howling and screaming like demons.

One Security officer threw down his rifle and burst into wild manic laughter. He flung himself on the ground and rolled there, screaming. MacAran, in split-second awareness, ran forward. He grabbed up the thrown-down gun; wrested another away from the second man, and ran toward the ship as the third Security man, who had only a handgun, fired. In MacAran's rocking brain the shot sounded like an infinite gallery of echoes, and with a wild high scream, one of the girls fell on the ground, rolling where she lay in agony.

MacAran, dragging the rifles, burst into the Captain's presence in the computer dome; Leicester raised his beetling brows, demanding explanation, and MacAran watched the eyebrows crawl up like caterpillars, take wing and flutter loose in the dome . . . *no*. NO! Fighting the spinning attack of unreality, he gasped, "Captain, it's happening again! What happened to us all on the slopes! For the love of God, lock up the guns and ammo before someone gets killed! One girl's already been shot—"

"*What?*" Leicester stared at him in frank disbelief. "Surely you're exaggerating . . ."

"Captain, I went through it," MacAran said, fighting desperately against the urge to fling himself down and roll on the floor, to grab the Captain by the throat and shake him to death. . . . "It's real. It's—you know Ewen Ross. You know he's had careful, complete Medic training—and he lay in the woods fooling around with Heather and MacLeod while a dying patient ran right past him and collapsed with a burst aorta. Camilla—Lieutenant Del Rey—threw away her telescope and ran off to chase butterflies."

"And you think this—this epidemic is going to strike here?"

"Captain, I *know* it," MacAran pleaded, "I'm—I'm fighting it off now—"

Leicester had not become Captain of a starship by being unimaginative or by refusing to meet emergencies. As the sound of a second shot erupted in the space before the clearing, he ran for the door, hitting an alarm button as he ran. When no one answered he shouted, running across the clearing.

MacAran, at his heels, sized up the situation in the flicker of an eye. The girl shot by the officer was still lying on the ground, writhing in pain; as they burst into the area Security men and the young people of the Commune were grappling hand to hand, shouting wild obscenities. A third shot rang out; one of the Security officers howled in pain and fell, clutching his kneecap.

"Danforth!" the Captain bellowed.

Danforth swung round, gun levelled, and for a split second MacAran thought he would pull the trigger again, but the years-long habit of obedience to the Captain made the berserk officer hesitate. Only a minute, but by that time MacAran's flying body struck him in a rough tackle; the man came crashing to the ground and the gun rolled away. Leicester dived for it, broke it, thrust the cartridges in his pocket.

Danforth struggled like a mad thing, clawing at MacAran, grappling for his throat; MacAran felt the surge of wild rage rising in him too, with spinning red colors before his eyes. He wanted to claw, to bite, to gouge out the man's eyes . . . with savage effort, remembering what had happened before, he brought himself back to reality and let the man rise to his feet. Danforth stared at the Captain and began to blubber, wiping his streaming eyes with doubled fists and muttering incoherently.

Captain Leicester snarled, "I'll break you for this, Danforth! Get to quarters!"

Danforth gave a final gulp. He relaxed and smiled lazily at his superior officer. "Captain," he murmured tenderly, "did anybody ever tell you that you got beautiful big blue eyes? Listen, why don't we—" straight-faced, smiling, in perfect seriousness, he made an obscene suggestion that made Leicester gasp, turn purple with rage, and draw breath to bellow at him again. MacAran grabbed the Captain's arm urgently.

"Captain, don't do anything you'll be sorry for. Can't you see he doesn't know what he's doing or saying?"

Danforth had already lost interest and ambled off, idly kicking at pebbles. Around them the nucleus of the fight had lost momentum; half the combatants were sitting on the ground crooning; the others had separated into little clumps of two and three. Some were simply stroking one another with total animal absorption and a complete lack of inhibitions, lying on the rough grass; others had already proceeded, totally without discrimination—man and woman, woman and woman, man and man—to more direct and active satisfactions. Captain Leicester stared at the daylight orgy in consternation and began to weep.

A surge of disgust flared up in MacAran, blotting out his early concern and compassion for the man. Simultaneously he was torn between reeling, struggling emotions; a rising surge of lust, so that he wanted to fall to the ground with the crowded, entwined bodies, a last scrap of compunction for the Captain—*he doesn't know what he's doing, not even as much as I do . . .* and a wave of rising sickness. Abruptly he bolted, sick panic blotting out everything else, stumbled and ran from the scene.

Behind him a long-haired girl, little more than a child, came up to the Captain, urged him down with his head on her lap, and rocked him like a baby, crooning softly in Gaelic. . . .

Ewen Ross saw and felt the first wave of rising unreason . . . it hit him as panic . . . and simultaneously, inside the hospital building, a patient still shrouded in bandages and comatose for days rose, ripped off his bandages and, while Ewen and a nurse stared in horrified consternation, tore his wounds open and laughing, bled to death. The nurse hurled a huge carboy of green soap at the dying man; then Ewen, fighting wildly for control of the waves of madness that threatened to overcome him (*the ground was rocking in earthquake, wild vertigo rippled his guts and head with nausea, insane colors spun before his eyes . . .*) leaped for the nurse and after a moment's struggle, took away the scalpel with which she was ripping at her wrists. He resisted her entwining arms (*throw her down on the bed now, tear her dress off . . .*) and ran for Dr. Di Asturien, to gasp out a terrified plea to lock up all poisons, narcotics and surgical instruments. Hastily drafting Heather (she had, after all, some memory of her own first attack) they managed to get more of them locked away and the key safely hidden before the whole hospital went berserk. . . .

Deep in the forest, the unaccustomed sunlight glazed the forest lawns and clearings with flowers and filled the air with pollen sweeping down from the heights on the wind.

Insects hurried from flower to flower, from leaf to leaf; birds mated, built nests of warm feathers with their eggs encased in insulating mud-and-straw walls, to hatch enclosed and feed on stored nectars and resins until the next warm spell. Grasses and grains scattered their seed, which the next snows would fertilize and moisten to sprout.

On the plains, the stag-like beasts ran riot, stampeding, fighting, coupling in broad daylight, as the pollen-laden winds sent their curious scents deep into the brain. And in the trees of the lower slopes, the small furred humanoids ran wild, venturing to the ground—some of them for the only time in their lives—feasting on the abruptly-ripening fruits, bursting through the clearings in maddened disregard of the prowling beasts. Generations and millennia of memory, in their genes and brains, had taught them that at this time, even their natural enemies were unable to sustain the long effort of chase.

Night settled over the world of the four moons; the dark sun sank in a strange clear twilight and the rare stars appeared. One after another, the moons climbed the sky; the great violet-gleaming moon, the paler green and blue gemlike discs, the small one like a white pearl. In the clearing where the great starship, alien to this world, lay huge and strange and menacing, the men from Earth breathed the strange wind and the strange pollen borne

90

on its breath, and curious impulses struggled and erupted in their forebrains.

Father Valentine and half a dozen strange crewmen sprawled in a thicket, exhausted and satiated.

In the hospital, fevered patients moaned untended, or ran wildly into the clearing and into the forest, in search of they knew not what. A man with a broken leg ran a mile through the trees before his leg gave way beneath him and he lay laughing in the moonlight while a tigerlike beast licked his face and fawned on him.

Judith Lovat lay quietly in her quarters, swinging the great blue jewel on the chain around her throat; she had kept it, all this time, concealed beneath her clothing. Now she drew it out, as if the strange starlike patterns within it exerted some hypnotic influence on her. Memories swirled in her mind, of the strange smiling madness that had been on her before. After a time, following some invisible call, she rose, dressed warmly, calmly appropriating her room-mate's warmest clothing (her room-mate, a girl named Eloise, who had been a communications officer on shipboard, was sitting under a longleafed tree, listening to the strange sounds of the wind in its leaves and singing wordlessly). Judy went calmly through the clearing, and struck into the forest. She was not sure where she was going, but she knew she would be guided when the time came, so she followed the upward trail, never deviating, listening to the music in the wind.

Phrases heard on another planet echoed dimly in her mind, *by woman wailing for her demon lover. . . .*

No, not a demon, she thought, *but too bright, too strange and beautiful to be human . . .* she heard herself sob as she walked, remembering the music, the shimmering winds and flowers, and the strange, glowing eyes of the half-remembered being, the clutch of fear that had quickly turned to enchantment and then to a happiness, a sense of closeness more intense than anything she had ever known.

Had it been something like this, then, those old Earth-legends of a wanderer lured away by the fairy-folk, the poet who had cried out in his enchantment:

> I met a Lady in the wood,
> A fairy's child

91

> Her hair was long, her foot was light
> And her eyes were wild. . . .

Was it like that? Or was it—*And the Son of God looked on the daughters of men, and beheld they were fair. . . .*

Judy was enough of a disciplined scientist to be aware that in the curious actions of this time there was something of madness. She was certain that some of her memories were colored and changed by the strange state of consciousness she had been in then. Yet experience and reality testing counted for something, too. If there was a touch of madness in it, behind the madness lay something real, and it was as real as the tangible touch on her mind now, that said, *"Come. You will be led, and you will not be harmed."*

She heard the curious rustle in the leaves over her head, and stopped, looking up, her breath catching in anticipation. So deep was her hope and longing to see the strange unforgotten face that she could have wept when it was only one of the little ones, the small red-eyed aliens, who peered at her shy and wild through the leaves, then slid down the trunk and stood before her, trembling and yet confident, holding out his hands.

She could not entirely reach his mind. She knew the little ones were far less developed than she, and the language barrier was great. Yet, somehow, they communicated. The small tree-man knew that she was the one he sought, and why; Judy knew that he had been sent for her, and that he bore a message she desperately hungered to hear. In the trees she saw other strange and shy faces, and in another moment, once they were aware of her good will, they slipped down and were all around her. One of them slid a small cool hand into her fingers; another garlanded her with bright leaves and flowers. Their manner was almost reverent as they bore her along, and she went with them without protest, knowing that this was only a prologue to the real meeting she longed for.

High in the wrecked ship an explosion thundered. The ground shook, and the echoes rolled through the forest, frightening the birds from the trees. They flew up in a cloud that darkened the sun for a moment, but no one in the clearing of the Earthmen heard. . . .

Moray lay outstretched on the soft ploughed soil of the garden unit, listening with a deep inner knowledge to the soft ways of growth of the plants embedded in the soil. It seemed to him, in those expanding moments, that he could hear the grass and leaves growing, that some of the alien Earth-plants were complaining, weeping, dying, while others, in this strange ground, throve and changed, their inner cells altering and changing as they must to adapt and survive. He could not have put any of this into words, and, a practical and materialistic man, he would never rationally believe in ESP. Yet, with the unused centers of his brain stimulated by the strange madness of this time, he did not try to rationalize or believe. He simply knew, and accepted the knowledge, and knew it would never leave him.

Father Valentine was awakened by the rising sun over the clearing. At first, dazed, and still flooded with the strange awarenesses, he sat staring in wonder at the sun and the four moons which, by some trick of the light or his curiously heightened senses, he could see quite clearly in the deep-violet sunrise; green, violet, alabaster-pearl, peacock-blue. Then memory came flooding in, and horror, as he saw the crewmen scattered around him, still deep in sleep, exhausted. The full hideous horror of what he had done, in those last hours of darkness and animal hungers, bore in on a mind too confused and hyperstimulated even to be aware of its own madness.

One of the crewmen had a knife in his belt. The little priest, his face streaming with tears, snatched it out and began very seriously expunging all the witnesses to his sin, muttering to himself the phrases of the last rites as he watched the streaming blood. . . .

It was the wind, MacAran thought. Heather had been right; it was something in the wind. Some substance, airborne, dust or pollen, which caused this madness to run riot. He had known it before, and this time he had had some idea what was happening; enough to work all through the early stages, swept only by recurrent attacks of sudden panic or euphoria, at locking up weapons, ammunition, poisons from the hospital or the chemistry lab. He knew that Heather and Ewen were doing the same thing, to some limited extent, in the hospital. But even so he was numbed with horror at the events of the last day and night, and when night fell, knowing rationally that one semi-sane man could do little against two hundred completely crazed men and women, he had simply hidden in the woods, desperately clinging to sanity against the recurrent waves of madness that clutched at him. This damned planet! This damned world, with the winds of madness that crept like ghosts from the towering hills, ravening madness that touched men and beasts alike. An encompassing, devouring, ghost wind of madness and terror!

The Captain is right. We've got to get off this world. No one can survive here, nothing human, we're too vulnerable ...

He was gripped with desperate anxiety for Camilla. In this mad night of rape, murder, panic terror out of control, savage battle and destruction, where had she gone? His earlier search for her had been fruitless, even though, aware of his heightened senses, he had tried to "listen" in that strange way which, on the mountain, had allowed him to find her unerringly through the blizzard. But his own fear acted like static blurring a sensitive receptor; he could feel her, but where? Had she hidden, like himself after he knew the hopelessness of his search, simply trying to escape the madness of the others? Had she been gripped by the lust and wild sensual euphoria of some of the others, and was she simply caught up in one of the groups madly pleasuring and indifferent to all else? The thought was agony to MacAran, but it was the safest alternative. It was the only bearable alternative—otherwise the thought that she might have met some murder-crazed crewman before the weapons were safely locked away, the fear that she might have run into the woods in a recurrence of panic and there been clawed or savaged by some animal, would have driven him quite witless with fear.

His head was buzzing, and he staggered as he walked across the clearing. In a thicket near the stream he saw motionless bodies—dead or wounded or sated, he could not tell; a quick glance told him Camilla was not there and he went on. The ground seemed to rock under his feet and it took all his concentration not to dash madly off into the trees, looking for . . . looking for . . . he wrenched himself back to awareness of his search and grimly went on.

Not in the recreation hall, where members of the New Hebrides Commune were sprawled in exhausted sleep or vacantly strumming musical instruments. Not in the hospital, although on the floor a snowstorm of paper showed him where someone had gone berserk with the medical records . . . *stoop down, scoop up a handful of paper scraps, sift them through your fingers like falling snow, let them whirl away on the wind* . . . MacAran never knew how long he stood there listening to the wind and watching the playing clouds before the wave of surging madness receded again, like a tidal wave dragging and sucking back from the shore. But the racing clouds had covered the sun, and the wind was blowing ice-cold by the time he recovered himself and began, in a wave of panic, hunting madly in every corner and clearing for Camilla.

He entered the computer dome last, finding it darkened (*what had happened to the lights! Had that explosion knocked them all out, all the power controls from the ship?*) and at first MacAran thought it was deserted. Then, as his eyes grew accustomed to the dim light, he made out shadowy figures back in the corner of the building; Captain Leicester, and—yes—Camilla, kneeling at his side and holding his hand.

By now he took it for granted that he was actually hearing the Captain's thoughts, *why have I never really seen you before, Camilla?* MacAran was amazed and in a small sane part of his mind, ashamed at the wave of primitive emotion that surged over him, a roaring rage that snarled in him and said, *this woman is mine!*

He came toward them, rising on the balls of his feet, feeling his throat swelling and his teeth drawn back and bared, his voice a wordless snarl. Captain Leicester sprang up and faced him, defiantly, and again with that odd, heightened sensitivity, MacAran was aware of the mistake the Captain was making . . .

Another madman, I must protect Camilla against him, that much duty I can still do for my crew . . . and coherent thought blurred out in a surge of rage and desire. It maddened MacAran; Leicester crouched and sprang at him, and the two men went down, gripping one another, roaring deep in their throats in primitive battle. MacAran came uppermost and in a flick of a moment he saw

95

Camilla lying back tranquilly against the wall; but her eyes were dilated and eager and he knew that she was excited by the sight of the struggling men, that she would accept—passively, not caring—whichever of them now triumphed in the fight—

Then a wash of sanity came over MacAran. He tore himself free of the Captain, struggling to his feet. He said, in a low, urgent voice, "Sir, this is idiotic. If you fight it, you can get out of this. Try to fight it, try to stay sane—"

But Leicester, rolling free, came up to his feet, snarling with rage, his lips flecked with foam and his eyes unfocused and quite mad. Lowering his head, he charged full steam at MacAran; Rafe, quite cool-headed now, stepped back. He said regretfully, "I'm sorry, Captain," and a well-aimed single blow to the point of the chin connected and knocked the crazed man senseless to the floor.

He stood looking down at him, feeling rage drain out of him like running water. Then he went to Camilla and knelt beside her. She looked up at him and smiled, and suddenly, in the way he could no longer doubt, they were in contact again. He said gently, "Why didn't you tell me you were pregnant, Camilla? I would have worried, but it would have made me very happy, too."

I don't know. At first, I was afraid, I couldn't accept it; it would have changed my life too much.

But you don't mind now?

She said aloud, "Not just at this minute, I don't mind, but things are so different now. I might change again."

"Then it isn't an illusion," MacAran said, half aloud, "we *are* reading each other's minds."

"Of course," she said, still with that tranquil smile, "didn't you know?"

Of course, then, MacAran thought; this is why the winds bring madness.

Primitive man on Earth must have had ESP, the whole gamut of psi powers, as a reserve survival power. Not only would it account for the tenacious belief in them against only the sketchiest proof, but it would account for survival where mere sapience would not. A fragile being, primitive man could not have survived without the ability to *know* (with his eyesight dimmer than the birds, his hearing less than a tenth of that of any dog or carnivore,) where he could find food, water, shelter; how to avoid natural enemies. But as he evolved civilization and technology, these unused powers were lost. The man who walks little, loses the ability to run and climb; yet the muscles are there and can be developed, as every athlete and circus performer learns. The man who relies on notebooks loses the ability of the old bards, to memorize daylong epics and genealogies. But for all these millennia the old ESP powers lay dormant in his genes and chromosomes, in his brain—and some chemical in the strange wind (pollen? dust? virus?) had restimulated it.

Madness, then. Man, accustomed to using only five of his senses, bombarded by new data from the unused others, and his primitive brain also stimulated to its height, could not face it, and reacted—some by total, terrifying loss of inhibition; some with ecstasy; some with blank, blind refusal to face the truth.

If we are to survive on this world, then, we must learn to listen to it; to face it; to use it, not to fight it.

Camilla took his hand. She said aloud, in a soft voice, "Listen, Rafe. The wind is dying; it will rain, soon, and this will be over. We may change—I may change again with the wind, Rafe. Let us enjoy being together now— while I can." Her voice sounded so sad that the man, too, could have wept. Instead, he took her hand and they walked quietly out of the dome; at the door Camilla paused, slipped her hand gently free of Rafe's and went back. She bent over the Captain, slid her rolled-up windbreaker gently under his head; knelt at his side for a moment and kissed his cheek. Then she rose and came back to Rafe, clinging to him, shaking softly with unshed tears, and he led her out of the dome.

High on the slopes, mists gathered and a soft fine foggy rain began to fall. The small red-eyed furred creatures, as if waking from a long dream, stared wildly about themselves and scurried for the safety of their tree-roads and shelters of woven wood and wicker. The cavorting beasts in the valleys bellowed softly in confusion and hunger, abandoned their cavorting and stampeding and began quietly to graze along the streams again. And, as if waking from a hundred long confused nightmares, the alien men from Earth, feeling the rain on their faces, the effects of the wind receding in their minds, woke and found that in many cases, the nightmare, acted out, was dreadfully real.

Captain Leicester came up slowly to consciousness in the deserted computer dome, hearing the sounds of rain beating in the clearing outside. His jaw ached; he struggled up to his feet, feeling his face ruefully, fighting for memory out of the strange confused thoughts of the past thirty-six hours or so. His face was furred with stubble, unshaven; his uniform filthy and mussed. Memory? He shook his head, confused; it hurt, and he put his hands to his throbbing temples.

Fragments spun in his mind, half real like a long dream. Gunfire, and a fight of some sort; the sweet face of a red-headed girl, and a sharp unmistakable memory of her body, naked and welcoming—had that been real or a wild fantasy? An explosion that had rocked the clearing—the ship? His mind was still too fuzzed with dream and nightmare to know what he had done or where he had gone after that, but he remembered coming back here to find Camilla alone, *of course she would protect the computer, like a mother hen her one chick,* and a vague memory of a long time with Camilla, holding her hand while some curious, deep-rooted communion went on, intense and complete, achingly close, yet somehow not sexual, although there had been that too—*or was that illusion, confused memory of the redheaded girl whose name he did not know*—the strange songs she had sung—and another surge of fear and protectiveness, an explosion in his mind, and then black darkness and sleep.

Sanity returned, a slow rise, a receding of the nightmare. What had been happening to the ship, to the crew, to the others, in this time of madness? He didn't know. He'd better find out. He vaguely remembered that someone had been shot, before he freaked out—or was that, too, part of the long madness? He pressed the button by which he summoned the ship's Security men, but there was no response and then he realized that the lights were not working, either. So someone had gotten to the power sources, in madness. What other damage? He'd better go and find out. Meanwhile, where was Camilla?

(At this moment she slipped reluctantly away from Rafe, saying gently, "I must go and see what damage has been done in the ship, *querido*. The Captain, too; remember I am still part of the crew. Our time is over—at least for now. There's going to be plenty for all of us to do. I must go to him—yes, I know, but I love him too, not as

98

I do you, but I'm learning a lot about love, my darling, and he may have been hurt.")

She walked across the clearing, through the blowing rain which was beginning to be mixed with heavy wet snow. *I hope someone finds some kind of fur-bearing animals,* she thought, *the clothes made for Earth won't face a winter here.* It was a quite routine thought at the back of her mind as she went into the darkened dome.

"Where have you been, Lieutenant?" the Captain said thickly. "I have a queer feeling I owe you some kind of apology, but I can't remember much."

She looked around the dome, quickly assessing damage. "It's foolish to call me Lieutenant here, you've called me Camilla before this—before we ever landed here."

"Where is everybody, Camilla? I suppose it's the same thing that hit you in the mountains?"

"I suppose so. I imagine before long we'll be up to our ears in the aftermath," she said with a sharp shudder. "I'm frightened, Captain—" she broke off with an odd little smile. "I don't even know your name."

"It's Harry," Captain Leicester said absent-mindedly, but his eyes were fixed on the computer and with a sudden, sharp exclamation Camilla went toward it. She found one of the resin-candles issued for lights and lit it, holding it up to examine the console.

The main banks of storage information were protected by plates from dust, damage, accidental erasure or tampering. She caught up a tool and began to unfasten the plates, working with feverish haste. The Captain came, caught up by her air of urgency, and said, "I'll hold the light." Once he had taken it, she moved faster, saying between her teeth, "Someone's been at the plates, Captain, I don't like this—"

The protective plate came away in her hands, and she stared, her face slowly whitening, her hands dropping to her sides in horror and dismay.

"You know what's happened," she said, her voice sticking in her throat. "It's the computer. At least half the programs—maybe more—have been erased. Wiped. And without the computer—"

"Without the computer," Captain Leicester said slowly, "the ship is nothing but a few thousand tons of scrap metal and junk. We're finished, Camilla. Stranded."

Chapter
TEN

High above the forest, in a close-woven shelter of wickerwork and leaves, the rain beating softly outside, Judy rested on a sort of dais covered with soft woven fabric and took in, not with words entirely, what the beautiful alien with the silver eyes was trying to tell her.

"Madness comes upon us too, and I am deeply sorrowful to have intruded into your people's lives this way. There was a time—not now, but lost in our history—when our folk travelled, as yours do, between the stars. It may even be that all men are of one blood, back in the beginning of time, and that your people too are our little brothers, as with the furred people of the trees. Indeed it would seem so, since you and I came together under the madness in the winds and now you bear this child. It is not that I regret, entirely—"

A feather's-touch upon her hand, no more, but Judy felt she had never known anything as tender as the sad eyes of the alien. *"Now, with no madness in my blood, I feel only deep grief for you, little one. No one of our own would be allowed to bear a child in loneliness, and yet you must return to your own people, we could not care for you. You could not even bear the cold of our dwelling-places in high summer, in winter you would surely die, my child."*

All of Judy's being was one great cry of anguish, *will I never see you again?*

I can reach you so clearly only at these times, the answer flowed, *although your mind is more open to me than before, the minds of your people are like half-shut doors at other times. It would be wisest for me to let you go now, for you never to look back to the time of madness, and yet*—long silence, and a great sigh. *I cannot, I cannot, how can I let you go from me and never know . . .*

The strange alien reached out, touching the jewel which hung about her neck on a fine chain, and drew it forth.

We use these—sometimes—for the training of our children. Mature, we do not need them. It was a love-gift to you; an act of madness, perhaps, perhaps unwise, my elders would certainly say so. Yet perhaps, if your mind is opened enough to master the jewel, perhaps I can reach you at times, and know that all is well with you and the child.

She looked at the jewel, which was blue, like a star-sapphire, with small inner flecks of fire, only a moment; then raised her eyes to look again with grief on the alien being. Taller than mortal, with great pale-grey eyes, almost silver, fair-skinned and delicate of feature, with long slender fingers and bare feet even in the bitter chill, and with long almost colorless hair floating like weightless silk about the shoulders; strange and bizarre and yet beautiful, with a beauty that struck at the woman like pain. With infinite tenderness and sadness, the alien reached for her and folded her very briefly against the delicate body, and she sensed that this was a rare thing, a strange thing, a concession to her despair and loneliness. *Of course. A telepathic race would have little use for demonstrative displays.*

And now you must go, my poor little one. I will take you to the edge of the forest, the Little Folk will guide you from there. (I fear your people, they are so violent and savage and your minds . . . your minds are closed . . .)

Judy stood looking up at the stranger, her own grief at parting blurring in the perception of the other's fear and anguish. "I understand," she whispered aloud, and the other's drawn face relaxed a little.

Shall I see you again?

There are so many chances, both for good and evil, child. Only time knows, I dare not promise you. With a gentle touch, he folded her in the fur-lined cloak in which, earlier, he had wrapped her. She nodded, trying to hold back her tears; only when he had disappeared into the forest did she break down and follow, weeping, the small furred alien who came to lead her down the strange paths.

"You are the logical suspect," Captain Leicester said harshly. "You have never made any secret of the fact that you don't want to leave this planet, and the sabotage of the computer means that you will get your way, and that we will never be able to leave here."

101

"No, Captain, you're quite wrong," Moray looked him in the face without flinching. "I have known all along that we would never leave this planet. It did occur to me, during the—what the hell shall we call it? During the mass freakout? Yes; it occurred to me during the mass freakout that maybe it would be a good thing if the computer was nonfunctional, it would force you to stop pretending we could fix the ship—"

"I was not *pretending*," said the Captain icily.

Moray shrugged. "Words don't matter that much. Okay, force you to stop kidding yourself about it, and get down to the serious business of survival. But I didn't do it. To be honest, I might have if it had ever occurred to me, but I don't know one end of a computer from the other—I wouldn't know how to go about putting it out of action. I suppose I *could* have blown it up—I know I heard the explosion—but as it happens, when I heard the explosion I was lying in the garden having—" suddenly he laughed, embarrassed, "having the time of my life talking to a cabbage sprout, or something like that."

Leicester frowned at him. He said, "Nobody blew the computer up, or even put it out of action. The programs have simply been erased. Any literate person could do that."

"Any literate person familiar with a starship, maybe," Moray said. "Captain, I don't know how to convince you, but I'm an ecologist, not a technician. I can't even make up a computer program. But if it's not out of commission, what's all the fuss about? Can't you re-program it, or whatever the word is? Are the tapes, or whatever they are, so irreplaceable?"

Leicester was abruptly convinced. Moray didn't *know*. He said dryly, "For your information, the computer contained about half of the sum total of human knowledge about physics and astronomy. Even if my crew contained four dozen Fellows of the Royal College of Astronomy of Edinburgh, it would take them thirty years to re-program just the navigational data. That's not even counting the medical programs—we haven't checked those yet—or any of the material from the ship's Library. All things considered, the sabotage of the computer is a worse piece of human vandalism than the burning of the Library at Alexandria."

"Well, I can only repeat that I didn't do it and I don't

know who did," Moray said. "Look for someone on your crew with the technical know-how." He gave a dry, unamused laugh. "And someone who could keep their head long enough. Have the Medics figured out what hit us?"

Leicester shrugged. "The best guess I've heard so far is an airborne dust containing some violent hallucinogen. Still unidentified, and probably will be until things settle down at the hospital."

Moray shook his head. He knew the Captain believed him now, and to tell the truth he was not entirely happy about the destruction of the computer. As long as Leicester's whole efforts were taken up in attempting to manage the ship repairs he was unlikely to interfere with what Moray was doing to assure the Colony's survival. Now, a Captain without a ship, he was likely to get seriously in the way of their assault on a strange world. For the first time Moray understood the old joke about the Space fleet:

"You can't retire a starship Captain. You have to shoot him."

The thought stirred dangerous fears in him. Moray was not a violent man, but during the thirty-six hours of the strange wind, he had discovered painful and unsuspected depths in himself. *Maybe someone else will think of that, next time—what makes me so sure there will be a next time? Or maybe I will, can I ever be sure now?*

Turning away from the unwelcome thought, he said, "Have you a report on damages yet?"

"Nineteen dead—no medical reports, but at least four hospital patients died of neglect," Leicester said shortly. "Two suicides. One girl cut herself and bled to death on broken glass, but probably accident rather than suicide. And—I suppose you heard about Father Valentine."

Moray shut his eyes. "I heard about the murders. I don't know all the details."

Leicester said, "I doubt if anyone alive does. He doesn't himself, and probably won't unless Chief Di Asturien wants to give him narcosynthesis or something. All I know is somehow he got mixed up with a gang of the crewmen who were doing some messing around—sexual messing around—down by the edge of the river. Things got fairly wild. When the first wave subsided a little he realized what he'd been doing, and I gather he couldn't face it, and started cutting throats."

"I take it, then, that he was one of the suicides?"

Leicester shook his head. "No. I gather he came out of it just in time to realize that suicide, too, was a mortal sin. Funny. I guess I'm just getting hardened to horrors on this wonderful paradise planet of yours—all I can think about now is how much trouble he'd have saved if he'd gone ahead with it. Now I've got to try him for murder, and then decide, or make the people decide, whether or not we have capital punishment here."

Moray smiled bleakly. "Why bother?" he said. "What verdict could you possibly get except *temporary insanity?*"

"My God, you're right!" Leicester passed his hand over his forehead.

"In all seriousness, Captain. We may have to cope with this again, and again, and again. At least until we know the cause. I suggest that you immediately disarm your Security crew; the first sign happened when a Security man shot first a girl, then a fellow officer. I suggest that if we ever again have a rainless night, that all lethal weapons, kitchen knives, surgical instruments, and the like, be locked up. It probably won't prevent all the trouble, we can't lock up every rock and hunk of stovewood on the planet, and to look at you, somebody evidently forgot who you were and took a swing at you."

Leicester rubbed his chin. "Would you believe a fight over a girl, at my age?"

For the first time the two men grinned at one another with the beginnings of a brief mutual human liking, then it receded. Leicester said, "I'll think about it. It won't be easy."

Moray said grimly, "Nothing here's going to be easy, Captain. But I have a feeling that unless we start up a serious campaign for an ethic of nonviolence—one that will hold even under stress like the mass freakout—none of us will live through the summer."

Chapter
ELEVEN

The days of the Wind had spared the garden, MacAran thought. Perhaps some deep survival-instinct had told the maddened colonists that this was their lifeline. Repairs to the hospital were underway, and work crews drafted for manual labor were doing salvage work on the ship— Moray had made it bitterly clear that for many years this would be their only stock of metal for tools and implements. Bit by bit, the interior fabric of the great starship was being cannibalized; furniture from the living quarters and recreation areas was being brought out and converted for use in the dormitory and community buildings, tools from the repair shops, kitchen areas and even the bridge decks were being inventoried by groups of clerical workers. MacAran knew that Camilla was busy checking the computer, trying to discover what programs had been salvaged. Down to the smallest implement, ball-point pens and women's cosmetics in the canteen supplies, everything was being inventoried and rationed. When the supplies of a technologically oriented Earth culture ran out, there would be no more, and Moray made it clear that replacements were already being devised for an orderly transition.

The clearing presented a curious blend, he thought; the small domes constructed with plastic and fiber, damaged in the blizzard and repaired with tougher local woods; the mixed piles of complex machinery, tended and guarded by uniformed crewmen with Chief Engineer Patrick in charge; the people from the New Hebrides Commune working—by their own choice, MacAran understood —in the garden and woods.

He held in his hand two slips of paper—the old habit of posting memoranda still held; he imagined that eventually dwindling paper supplies would phase it out. What would they substitute? Systems of bells coded to each person, as was done in some large department stores to attract the attention of a particular person? Word of mouth messages? Or would they manage to discover some way to make paper of local products and continue their centuries-long reliance on written memoranda? One of the slips he held told him to check in at the hospital for what was called routine examination; the other asked him to report to Moray's office for work analysis and assignment.

By and large, the announcement that the computer was useless and the ship perforce abandoned had been greeted without much outcry. One or two crewmen had been heard to mutter that whoever did it should be lynched, but there was at the moment no way of discovering either who had wiped the Navigation tapes from the computer, nor of finding out who had dynamited one of the inner drive chambers with an improvised bomb. Suspicion for the latter fell by default on a crewmember who had recently asked admission into the New Hebrides Commune and whose mangled body had been found inside the ship near the explosion site; and everyone was content to let it stay there.

MacAran suspected that the quiet was temporary, the result of shock, and that sooner or later there would be fresh storms, but for the moment everyone had simply accepted the urgent necessity to join together to repair damages and assure survival against the unguessed harshness of the unknown winter. MacAran himself was not sure how he felt about it, but he had in any case been ready for a colony, and secretly it seemed to him that it might be more interesting to colonize a "wild" planet than one extensively terraformed and worked over by Earth Expeditionary. But he hadn't been prepared to be cut off from the mainstream of Earth—no starships, no contact or communication with the rest of the Galaxy, perhaps for generations, perhaps forever. *That* hurt. He hadn't accepted it yet; he knew he might never accept it.

He went into the building where Moray's office was located, read the sign on the door (DON'T KNOCK, COME IN) and went in to find Moray talking to an unknown girl who must be, from her dress, one of the New Hebrides people.

"Yes, yes, dear, I know you want a work assignment to the garden, but your history shows you worked in art and ceramics and we're going to need you there. Do you realize that the first craft developed in almost every civilization is pottery? In any case, didn't I see a report that you were pregnant?"

"Yes, the Annunciation Ceremony for me was yesterday. But our kind of people always work right up to delivery."

Moray smiled faintly. "I'm glad you feel well enough to go on working. But women in colonies are never permitted to do manual work."

"Article four—"

"Article four," said Moray, and his face was grim, "was developed for Earth, Earth conditions. Get wise to the facts of life on planets with alien gravity, light and oxygen content, Alanna. This planet is one of the lucky ones; oxygen on the high side, light gravity, no anoxic or crush-syndrome babies. But even on the best planets, just the *change* does it, and it's a grim statistic for a population as low as ours. Half the women are sterile for five to ten years, half the fertile women miscarry for five to ten years. And half the live births die before they're a month old for five to ten years. Colony women have to be *pampered*, Alanna. Co-operate, or you'll be sedated and hospitalized. If you want to be one of the lucky ones with a live baby instead of a messed-up dead one, *co-operate*, and start doing it *now*."

When she had gone away with a slip for the hospital, looking dazed and shocked, MacAran took her place before the cluttered desk, and Moray grimaced up at him. "I take it you heard that. How'd you like *my* job—scaring the hell out of young pregnant girls?"

"Not much." MacAran was thinking of Camilla, also carrying a child. So she was not sterile. But one chance in two that she would miscarry—and then a fifty-fifty chance that her child would die. Grim statistics, and they sent a clutch of horror through him. Had she been advised of this? Did she know? Was she co-operating? He didn't know; she had been locked up with the Captain, hovering over the computer, for half the last tenday.

Moray said, frowning slightly, "Come out of the clouds. You're one of the lucky ones, MacAran—you're not technologically unemployed."

"Huh?"

"You're a geologist and we need you doing what you were trained for. You heard me tell Alanna that one of the first industries we need, in a hurry, at that, is *pottery*. For pottery, you need china clay, or a good substitute for it. We also need reliable building stone—we need concrete or cement of some sort—we need limestone, or something with the same properties; and we need silicates for glass, various ores . . . in fact, what we need is a geological assay of this part of the planet, and we need it before the winter sets in. You aren't priority one, Mac —but you're in category two or three. Can you draw up a plan for an assay and exploration in the next day or two, and tell me roughly how many men you'll need for sampling and testing?"

"Yes, I can do that easy enough. But I thought you said we couldn't go in for a technological civilization. . . ."

"We can't," Moray told him, "not as Engineer Patrick uses the word. No heavy industry. No mechanized transport. But there's no such thing as a non-technological civilization. Even the cave men had technology—they manufactured flints, or didn't you ever see one of their factory sites? Man is a tool-user—a technician. I never had any notion of starting us out as savages. The question is, *which* technologies can we manage, especially during the first three or four generations?"

"You plan that far ahead?"

"I have to."

"You said my job wasn't priority one. What's priority one?"

"Food," Moray said realistically. "Again, we're lucky. The soil's arable here—although I suspect marginally, so we're going to have to use fertilizers and composts—and agriculture *is* possible. I've known planets where the food-securing priority would have taken up so much time that even minimal *crafts* might have to be postponed for two or three generations. Earth doesn't colonize them, but we could have been marooned on one. There may even be domesticable animals here; MacLeod's on that now. Priority two is shelter—and by the way, when you make that survey, check some lower slopes for *caves*. They may be warmer than anything we can build, at least during the winter. After food and shelter come simple crafts—the amenities of life; weaving, pottery, fuel and lights, clothing, music, garden tools, furniture. You get the idea. Go draw up your survey, MacAran, and I'll assign you enough men to carry it out." He gave another of those grim smiles.

"Like I say; you're one of the lucky ones. This morning I've got to tell a deep-space communications expert with absolutely no other skills, that his job is completely obsolete for at least ten generations, and offer him a choice of agriculture, carpentry, or blacksmithing!"

As MacAran left the office, his thoughts flew again, compulsively, to Camilla. Was this what lay in store for her? No, certainly not, any civilized group of people must have some use for a computer library of information! But would Moray, with his grim priorities, see it that way?

He walked through the midday sunlight, pale violet shadows, the sun hanging high and red like an inflamed and bloodshot eye, toward the hospital. In the distance a solitary figure was toiling over rocks, building a low fence, and MacAran looked at Father Valentine, doing his solitary penance. MacAran accepted, in principle, the theory that the colony could spare no single pair of hands; that Father Valentine could atone for his crimes by useful work more easily than by hanging by the neck until dead; and MacAran, with the memory of his own madness lying heavy on him *(how easily he could have killed the Captain, in his rage of jealousy!)* could not even find it in his heart to shun the priest or feel horror at him. Captain Leicester's judgment would have done justice to King Solomon; Father Valentine had been commanded to bury the dead, those he had killed, and the others, to create a graveyard, and enclose it with a fence against wild beasts or desecration, and to build a suitable memorial to the mass grave of those who had died in the crash. MacAran was not certain what useful purpose a graveyard would serve, except perhaps to remind the Earthmen of how near death lay to life, and how near madness lay to sanity. But this work would keep the Father away from the other crewmen and colonists, who might not have the same awareness of how near they might have come to repeating his crime, until the memory had mercifully died down a little; and would provide enough hard work and penance to satisfy even the despairing man's need for punishment.

Somehow the sight of the lonely, bent figure put him out of the mood to keep his other appointment in the hospital. He walked away toward the woods, passing the garden area where New Hebrideans were tending long rows of green sprouting plants. Alastair, on his knees, was transplanting small green shoots from a flat screened pan; he returned MacAran's wave with a smile. *They were happy at the outcome of this, this life would suit them perfectly.* Alastair spoke a word to the boy holding the box of plants, got up and loped toward MacAran.

"The *padrón*—Moray—told me you were going to do geological work. What's the chances of finding materials for glassmaking?"

"Can't say. Why?"

"Climate like this, we need greenhouses," Alastair said, "concentrated sunlight. Something to protect young plants against blizzards. I'm doing what I can with plastic sheets, foil reflectors and ultraviolet, but that's a temporary make-shift. Check natural fertilizers and nitrates, too. The soil here isn't too rich."

"I'll make a note of it," MacAran promised. "Were you a farmer by trade on Earth?"

"Lord, no. Auto mechanic—transit specialist," Alastair grimaced. "The Captain was talking about converting me to a machinist. I'm going to be sittin' up nights praying for whoever it was blew up the damn ship."

"Well, I'll try to find your silicates," MacAran promised, wondering how high, on Moray's austere priorities, the art of glassmaking would come. And what about musical instruments? Fairly high, he'd imagine. Even savages had music and he couldn't imagine life without them, nor, he'd guess, could these members of a singing folk.

If the winter's as bad as it probably will be, music just might keep us all sane, and I'll bet that Moray— cagey bastard that he is—has that already figured out.

As if in answer to his thought, one of the girls working in the field raised her voice in low, mournful song. Her voice, deep and husky, had a superficial resemblance to Camilla's, and the words of the song rang out, in question and sadness, an old sad melody of the Hebrides:

> My Caristiona,
> Wilt answer my cry?
> No answering tonight?
> My grief, ah me . . .
> My Caristiona . . .

Camilla, why do you not come to me, why do you not answer me? Wilt answer my cry . . . my grief, ah me . . .

Deep my heart is grieving, grieving,
And my eyes are streaming, streaming . . .
My Caristiona . . . wilt answer my cry?

*I know you are unhappy, Camilla, but why, why do you
not come to me . . . ?*

Camilla came into the hospital slowly and rebelliously,
clutching the examination slip. It was a comforting hang-
over from ship routine, but when, instead of the familiar
face of Medic Chief Di Asturien *(at least he speaks
Spanish!)* she was confronted with young Ewen Ross, she
frowned with irritation.

"Where's the Chief? You haven't the authority to do
examinations for Ship personnel!"

"The Chief's operating on that man who was shot in
the kneecap during the Ghost Wind; anyway I'm in charge
of routine examinations, Camilla. What's the matter?" His
round young face was ingratiating, "won't I do? I assure
you my credentials are wonderful. Anyhow, I thought we
were friends—fellow victims from the first of the Winds!
Don't damage my self-esteem!"

Against her will she laughed. "Ewen, you rascal, you're
impossible. Yes, I guess this is routine. The Chief an-
nounced the contraceptive failure a couple of months ago,
and I seem to have been one of the victims. It's just a
case of putting in for an abortion."

Ewen whistled softly. "Sorry, Camilla," he said gently,
"can't be done."

"But I'm *pregnant!*"

"So congratulations or something," he said, "maybe
you'll have the first child born here, or something, unless
one of the Commune girls gets ahead of you."

She heard him, frowning, not quite understanding. She
said stiffly, "I guess I'll have to take it up with the Chief
after all; you evidently don't understand the rules of the
Space Service."

His eyes held a deep pity; he understood all too well.
"Di Asturien would give you the same answer," he said
gently. "Surely you know that in the Colonies abortions
are performed only to save a life, or prevent the birth of a
grossly defective child, and I'm not even sure we have
facilities for *that* here. A high birth rate is absolutely
imperative for at least the first three generations—you

111

surely know that women volunteers aren't even accepted for Earth Expeditionary unless they're childbearing age and sign an agreement to have children?"

"I would be exempt, even so," Camilla flashed, "although I didn't volunteer for the colony at all; I was crew. But you know as well as I do that women with advanced scientific degrees are exempt—otherwise no woman with a career she valued would ever go out to the colonies! I'm going to fight this, Ewen! Damn you, I'm not going to accept forced childbearing! No woman is *forced* to have a child!"

Ewen smiled ruefully at the angry woman. He said, "Sit down, Camilla; be sensible. In the first place, love, the very fact that you have an advanced degree makes you valuable to us. We need your genes a lot more than we need your engineering skills. We won't be needing skills like that for half a dozen generations—if then. But genes for high intelligence and mathematical ability have to be preserved in the gene pool, we can't risk letting them die out."

"Are you trying to tell me I'll be *forced* to have children? Like some savage woman, some walking womb from the prehistoric planets?" Her face was white with rage. "This is completely unendurable! Every woman on the crew will go out on strike when they hear that!"

Ewen shrugged. "I doubt it," he said. "In the first place, you've got the law wrong. Women are not allowed to volunteer for colonies unless they have intact genes, are of childbearing age and sign an agreement to have children—but women *over* childbearing age are *occasionally* accepted if they have medical or scientific degrees. Otherwise the end of your fertile years means the end of your chance to be accepted for a Colony—and do you know how long the waiting lists are for the Colonies? I waited four years; Heather's parents put her name down when she was ten, and she's twenty-three. The Over-population laws on Earth mean that some women have been on waiting lists for twelve years to have a *second* child."

"I can't imagine why they'd bother," Camilla said in disgust. "One child ought to be enough for any woman, if she has anything above the neck, unless she's a real neurotic with no independent sense of self-esteem."

"Camilla," Ewen said very gently, "this is biological. Even back in the 20th century, they did experiments on rats and ghetto populations and things, and found that one of the first results of crucial social overcrowding was the failure of maternal behavior. It's a pathology. Man is a rationalizing animal, so sociologists called it "Women's Liberation" and things like that, but what it amounted to was a pathological reaction to overpopulation and overcrowding. Women who couldn't be allowed to have children, had to be given some other work, for the sake of their mental health. But it wears off. Women sign an agreement, when they go to the colonies, to have a minimum of two children; but most of them, once they're out of the crowding of Earth, recover their mental and emotional health, and the average Colony family is four children—which is about right, psychologically speaking. By the time the baby comes, you'll probably have normal hormones too, and make a good mother. If not, well, it will at least have your genes, and we'll give it to some sterile woman to bring up for you. Trust me, Camilla."

"Are you trying to tell me that I've *got* to have this baby?"

"I sure as hell am," Ewen said, and suddenly his voice went hard, "and others too, provided you can carry them to term. There's a one in two chance that you'll have a miscarriage." Steadily, unflinching, he rehearsed the statistics which MacAran had heard from Moray earlier that same day. "If we're lucky, Camilla, we have fifty-nine fertile women now. Even if they all became pregnant this year, we'll be lucky to have twelve living children . . . and the viable level for this colony to survive means we've got to bring our numbers up to about four hundred before the oldest women start losing their fertility. It's going to be touch and go, and I have a feeling that any woman who refuses to have as many children as she can physically manage, is going to be awfully damned unpopular. Public Enemy Number One isn't in it."

Ewen's voice was hard, but with the heightened sensitivity he had known ever since the first Wind blasted him wide open to the emotions of others, he realized the hideous pictures that were spinning in Camilla's mind:

not a person, just a thing, a walking womb, a thing used for breeding, my mind gone, my skills useless . . . just a brood mare . . .

"It won't be that bad," he said in deep sympathy. "There will be plenty for you to do. But that's the way

113

it's got to be, Camilla. I'm sure it's worse for you than it is for some others, but it's the same for everyone. Our survival depends on it." He looked away from her; he could not face the blast of her agony.

She said, her lips tightening to a hard line, "Maybe it would be better *not* to survive, under conditions like that."

"I won't discuss that with you until you're feeling better," Ewen said quietly, "it's not worth the breath. I'll set up a prenatal examination for you with Margaret—"

"—I *won't!*"

Ewen got quickly to his feet. He signalled to a nurse behind her back and gripped her wrist in a hard grip, immobilizing her. A needle went into her arm; she looked at him with angry suspicion, her eyes already glazing slightly.

"What—"

"A harmless sedative. Supplies are short, but we can spare enough to keep you calmed down," Ewen said calmly. "Who's the father, Camilla? MacAran?"

"None of your affair!" she spat at him.

"Agreed, but I ought to know, for genetic records. Captain Leicester?"

"MacAran," she said with a surge of dull anger, and suddenly, with a deep gnawing pain, she remembered . . . *how happy they had been during the Winds* . . .

Ewen looked down at her senseless form with deep regret. "Get hold of Rafael MacAran," he said, "have him with her when she comes out of it. Maybe he can talk some sense into her."

"How can she be so selfish?" the nurse said in horror.

"She was brought up on a space satellite," Ewen said, "and in the Alpha colony. She joined the space service at fifteen and all her life she's been brainwashed into thinking childbearing was something she shouldn't be interested in. She'll learn. It's only a matter of time."

But secretly he wondered how many women of the crew felt the same—sterility could be psychologically determined too—and how long it would take to overcome this conditioned fear and aversion.

Could it even be done, in time to bring them up to a viable number, on this harsh, brutal and inhospitable world?

Chapter
TWELVE

MacAran sat beside the sleeping Camilla, thinking back over the hospital interview just past with Ewen Ross. After explaining about Camilla, Ewen had asked him only one further question:

"Do you remember having sex with anyone else during the Wind? I'm not just being idly curious, believe me. Some women, and some men, simply can't remember, or named at least half a dozen. By putting together everything that anyone *does* remember, we can eliminate certain people; that is, for genetic records later on. For instance, if some woman names three men as *possibly* responsible for her pregnancy, we only need to blood-test three men to establish—within rough limits, that is—the actual father."

"Only Camilla," MacAran said, and Ewen had grinned. "At least you're consistent. I hope you can talk that girl into some sense."

"I can't somehow see Camilla as much of a mother," MacAran said slowly, feeling disloyal, and Ewen shrugged. "Does it matter? We're going to have plenty of women either wanting children and unable to have them, miscarrying during pregnancy, or losing them at birth. If she doesn't want the child when it's born, one thing we're *not* going to be short of is foster mothers!"

Now that thought stirred Rafael MacAran to a slow resentment as he sat watching the drugged girl. The love between them, even at best, had arisen out of hostility, been an up-and-down thing of resentment and desire, and now the anger got out of control. *Spoiled brat,* he thought, *she's had everything her own way all her life, and now at the first hint she might have to give way to some consideration other than her own convenience, she starts making a fuss! Damn her!*

As if the violence of his angry thoughts had penetrated the thinning veils of the drug, Camilla's blue eyes, fringed

115

by heavy dark lashes, flicked open, and she looked around, in momentary bewilderment, at the translucent walls of the hospital dome, and MacAran by the side of her cot.

"Rafe?" A look of pain flicked over her face, and MacAran thought, *at least she's not calling me MacAran any more.* He spoke as gently as he could. "I'm sorry you're not feeling well, love. They asked me to come and sit with you a while."

Her face hardened as memory came back; he could feel her anger and misery and it was like pain inside him, and it turned off his own resentment like a switch being turned.

"I really am sorry, Camilla. I know you didn't want this. Hate me, if you've got to hate someone. It's my fault; I wasn't acting very responsibly, I know."

His gentleness, his willingness to take all the blame, disarmed her. "No, Rafe," she said painfully, "that's not fair to you. At the time it happened I wanted it as much as you did, so there's no point in blaming you. The trouble is, we've all gotten out of the *habit* of connecting pregnancy and sex, we all have a civilized attitude about it now. And of course none of us could have been *expected* to know that the regular contraceptives weren't working."

Rafe reached out to touch her hand. "Well, we'll share the blame, then. But can't you try to remember how you felt about it during the Wind? We were so happy then."

"I was *insane* then. So were you." The deep bitterness in her voice made him flinch with pain, not only for himself but for her. She tried to pull her hand free, but he held on to the slim fingers.

"I'm sane now—at least I think I am—and I still love you, Camilla. I haven't words to tell you how much."

"I should think you'd hate me."

"I couldn't hate you. I'm not happy that you don't want this child," he added, "and if we were on Earth I'd probably admit that you had a right to choose—not to bear it, if you didn't want to. But I wouldn't be happy about that either, and you can't expect me to be sorry that it's going to have a chance to live."

"So you're glad I'm going to be trapped into bearing it?" she flung at him, furious.

"How can I be glad about anything that makes you so miserable?" MacAran demanded in despair. "Do you think

116

I get any satisfaction out of seeing you unhappy? It tears me up, it's killing me! But you're pregnant, and you're sick, and if it makes you feel any better to say these things—I love you, and what can I do about it, except listen and wish I could say something helpful? I only wish you felt happier about it, and I wasn't so completely helpless."

Camilla could feel his confusion and distress as if they were her own, and this persistence of an effect she had associated only with the time of the winds shocked her out of her anger and self-pity. Slowly, she sat up in bed and reached for his hand.

"It's not your fault, Rafe," she said softly, "and if it makes you so unhappy for me to act like this, I'll try to make the best of it. I can't pretend I *want* a child, but if I have to have one—and it seems I do—I'd rather it was yours than someone else's." She smiled faintly, and added, "I suppose—the way things were going then—it could have been anyone, but I'm glad it was you."

Rafe MacAran found himself unable to speak—and then realized he didn't have to. He bent down and kissed her hand. "I'll do everything I can to make it easier," he promised, "and I only wish it were more."

Moray had finished work assignments for most of the colonists and crew by the time Chief Engineer Laurence Patrick found himself, with Captain Leicester, consulting the Colony Representative.

Patrick said, "You know, Moray, long before I became a M-AM drive expert I was a specialist in small all-terrain craft. There's enough metal in the ship, salvaged, to create several such craft, and they could be powered with small converted drive units. It would be a tremendous help to you in locating and structuring the resources of the planet, and I'm willing to handle the building. How soon can I get to it?"

Moray said, "Sorry, Patrick, not in your lifetime or mine."

"I don't understand. Wouldn't it help a great deal in exploring, and in maximizing use of resources? Are you *trying* to create as savage and barbarian an environment as you can possibly manage?" Patrick demanded angrily. "Lord help us, has the Earth Expeditionary become nothing but a nest of anti-technocrats and neo-ruralists?"

Moray shook his head, unruffled. "Not at all," he said. "My first colony assignment was on a planet where I designed a highly technical civilization based on maximal use of electric power and I'm extremely proud of it—in fact, I'm intending, or in view of our mutual catastrophe I should say I *had* been intending, to go back there at the end of my days and retire. My assignment to the Coronis colony meant I was designing technological cultures. But as things turned out—"

"It's still possible," said Captain Leicester. "We can pass down our technological heritage to our children and grandchildren, Moray, and some day, even if we're marooned here for life, our grandchildren will go back. Don't you know your history, Moray? From the invention of the steamboat to man's landing on the Moon was less than two hundred years. From there to the M-AM drives which landed us on Alpha Centauri, less than a hundred. We may all die on this Godforsaken lump of rock, we probably *will*. But if we can preserve our technology intact, enough to take our grandchildren back into the mainstream of human civilization, we won't be dying for nothing."

Moray looked at him with a deep pity. "Is it possible that you still don't understand? Let me spell it out for you, Captain, and you, Patrick. This planet will not support *any* advanced technology. Instead of a nickel-iron core, the major metals are low-density non-conductors, which explains why the gravity is so low. The rock, as far as we can tell without sophisticated equipment we don't have and can't build, is high in silicates but low in metallic ores. Metals are always going to be rare here—terrifyingly rare. The planet I spoke about, with enormous use of electric power, had huge fossil-fuel deposits *and* huge amounts of mountain streams to convert energy . . . *and* a very tough ecological system. This planet appears to be only marginally agricultural land, at least here. The forest cover is all that keeps it from massive erosion, so we must harvest timber with the greatest care, and preserve the forests as a lifeline. Added to that, we simply can't spare enough manual labor to build the vehicles you want, to service and maintain them, or to build such small roadways as they would need. I can give you exact facts and figures if you like, but in brief, if you insist on a mechanized technology you're handing

118

down a death sentence—if not for all of us, at least for our grandchildren; we might make it through three generations, because with such small numbers we could move on to a new part of the planet when we'd burned out one area. But no more."

Patrick said with deep bitterness, "Is it worth while surviving, or even *having* grandchildren, if they're going to live this way?"

Moray shrugged. "I can't make you have grandchildren," he said. "But I have a responsibility to the ones already on the way, and there are colonies without advanced technology which have just as long a waiting list as the one planned around massive use of electricity. Our lifeline isn't you people, I'm sorry to say; you are—to put it bluntly, Chief—just so much dead weight. The people we need on this world are the ones in the New Hebrides Commune—and I suspect if we survive at all, it's going to be their doing."

"Well," Captain Leicester said, "I guess that tells us where we stand." He thought it over a minute. "What's ahead for us, then, Moray?"

Moray looked at the records, and said, "I note on your personnel printout that your hobby at the academy was building musical instruments. That isn't very high priority, but this winter we can use plenty of people who know something about it. Meanwhile, do you know anything about glass blowing, practical nursing, dietetics, or elementary teaching?"

"I joined the service as a Medical Corpsman," Patrick said surprisingly, "before I went into Officer's Training."

"Go talk to Di Asturien in the hospital, then. For the time being I'll mark you down as assistant orderly, subject to drafts of all able-bodied men in the building program. An engineer should be able to handle architectural work and designing. As for you, Captain—"

Leicester said irritably, "It's idiotic to call me *Captain*. Captain of *what*, for God's sake, man!"

"Harry, then," Moray said, with a small wry grin. "I suspect titles and things will just quietly disappear within three or four years, but I'm not going to deprive anyone of one, if he wants to keep it."

"Well, consider I've phased mine out," Leicester said. "Going to draft me to hoe in the garden? Once I'm out as a spaceship captain, it's all I'm good for."

"No," Moray said bluntly. "I'm going to need whatever it was in you that made you a Captain—leadership, maybe."

"Any law against salvaging what technological know-how we have? Programming it into the computer, maybe, for those hypothetical grandchildren of ours?"

"Not so hypothetical in your case," Moray said, "Fiona MacMorair—she's over in the hospital as 'possible early pregnancy'—gave us your name as the probable father."

"Who the *hell,* pardoning the expression, who on this hell-fired world is Fiona Macwhatsis?" Leicester scowled. "I never heard of the damn girl."

Moray chuckled. "Does that matter? I happened to spend most of this wind making love to cabbage sprouts and baby bean plants, or at least listening to them telling me their troubles, but most of us spent it a little less— seriously, shall we say. Dr. Di Asturien's going to ask you the names of any possible female contacts."

Leicester said, "The only one I remember, I had to fight for, and I lost." He rubbed the fading bruise on his chin. "Oh, wait—is this a red-headed girl, one of the Commune group?"

Moray said, "I don't know the girl by sight. But about three-fourths of the New Hebrides people are red-haired— they're mostly Scots, and a few Irish. I'd say the chances were better than average that unless the girl miscarries, you'll have a red-headed son or daughter come nine-ten months from now. So you see, Leicester, you have a stake in this world."

Leicester flushed, a slow angry blush. He said, "I don't want my descendants to live in caves and scratch the ground for a living. I want them to know what kind of world we came from."

Moray did not answer for a moment. Finally he said, "I ask you seriously—don't answer, I'm not the keeper of your conscience, but think it over—might it not be best to let our descendants evolve a technology indigenous to this world? Rather than tantalizing them with the knowledge of one that could destroy this planet?"

"I'm counting on my descendants having good sense," Leicester said.

"Go ahead and program the stuff into the computer, then, if you want to," Moray said with the same small shrug, "maybe they'll have too much good sense to use it."

Leicester turned to go. "Can I have my assistant back? Or has Camilla Del Rey been assigned to something *important*, like cooking or making curtains for the hospital?"

Moray shook his head. "You can have her back when she's out of the hospital," he said, "although I've got her listed as pregnant, for assignment to light work only, and I thought we'd ask her to write some elementary mathematics texts. But the computer isn't very strenuous; if she wants to go back to it, I've no objection."

He looked pointedly at the work charts cluttering his desk, and Harry Leicester, ex-captain of the starship, realized that he had been, for all practical purposes, dismissed.

Chapter
THIRTEEN

Ewen Ross hesitated over the genetic charts and looked up at Judith Lovat. "Believe me, Judy. I'm not trying to make trouble for you, but it's going to make our records a lot simpler. Who was the father?"

"You didn't believe me when I told you before," Judy said flatly, "so if you know the answer better than I do, say whatever you like."

"I hardly know how to answer you," Ewen said. "I don't remember being with you, but if you say I was—"

She shook her head stubbornly, and he sighed. "The same story of an alien. Can't you see how fantastic that is? How completely unbelievable? Are you trying to postulate that the aborigines of this world are human enough to crossbreed with our women?" He hesitated. "You aren't by any chance being funny, Judy?"

"I'm not postulating anything, Ewen. I'm not a geneticist, I'm simply an expert in dietetics. I'm simply telling you what happened."

"During a time when you were insane. Two times."

121

Heather touched his arm gently. "Ewen," she said, "Judy's not lying. She's telling the truth—or what she believes to be the truth. Take it easy."

"But damn it, her beliefs aren't evidence." Ewen sighed and shrugged. "All right, Judy, have it your way. But it must have been MacLeod—or Zabal. Or me. Whatever you think you remember, it must have been."

"If you say so, of course it must have been," Judy said, quietly stood up and walked away, knowing without needing to look that what Ewen had written down was *father unknown; possible: MacLeod, Lewis; Zabal, Marco; Ross, Ewen.*

Heather said quietly behind the closing door, "Darling, you were a little rough on her."

"I happen not to think we have room for fantasy on a world as rough as this. Damn it, Heather, I was trained to save life at all costs—*all* costs. And I've already had to see people die . . . I've *let* them die—when we're sane, we've got to be *supersane* to compensate!" the young doctor said wildly.

Heather thought about that for a minute and finally said, "Ewen, how do you judge? Maybe what seems sanity on Earth might be foolishness here. For instance, you know the Chief is training groups of the women for pre-natal care and midwifery—in case, he says, we lose too many people this winter for the Medical staff to cope. He also said that he himself hadn't delivered a baby since he was an intern—you don't in the Space Service of course. Well, one of the first things he told us was; if a woman's going to miscarry, don't take any extraordinary measures to prevent it. If having the mother rest and keep warm won't save the child, nothing else; no hormones, no fetal-support drugs, nothing."

"That's fantastic," Ewen said, "it's almost criminal!"

"That's what Dr. Di Asturien said," Heather told him. "On Earth, it *would* be criminal. But here, he said, first of all, a threatened miscarriage may be one way of nature discarding an embryo which can't adapt to the environment here—gravity, and so forth. Better to let the woman miscarry early and start over, instead of wasting six months carrying a child who will die, or grow up defective. Also, on Earth, we could afford to save defective children—lethal genes, mental retardates, congenital deformities, fetal insults, and so forth. We had elaborate

122

machinery and medical structure for such things as exchange transfusions, growth-hormone transplants, rehabilitation and training if the child grew up defective. But here, unless some day we want to take the harsh step of exposing defective infants or killing them, we'd better keep them down to an absolute minimum—and about half the defective children born on Earth—maybe ninety per cent, nobody knows, it's such routine now on Earth to prevent a miscarriage at any cost—are the result of preventing children who really should have died, nature's mistakes, from being selected out. On a world like this, it's absolute survival for our race; we can't let lethal genes and defects get into our gene pool. See what I mean? Insanity on Earth—harsh facts for survival here. Natural selection has to take its course—and this means no heroic methods to prevent miscarriages, no extreme methods to save moribund or birth-damaged babies."

"And what's all this got to do with Judy's wild story about an alien being fathering her child?" Ewen demanded.

"Only this," Heather said, "we've got to learn to think in new ways—and not to reject things out of hand because they sound fantastic."

"You *believe* some nonhuman alien—oh, come, Heather! For God's sake!"

"What God?" Heather asked. "All the Gods I ever heard of belong to Earth. I don't *know* who fathered Judy's baby. I wasn't there. But she was, and in the absence of proof about it, I'd take *her* word. She's not a fanciful woman, and if she says that some alien came along and made love to her, and that she found herself pregnant, damn it, I'll believe it until it's proved otherwise. At least until I see the baby. If it's the living image of you, or Zabal, or MacLeod, maybe I'll believe Judy had a brainstorm. But during this second Wind, you behaved rationally, up to a point. MacAran behaved rationally, up to a point. Evidently after the first exposure, a *little* control remains on subsequent exposures to the drug, or pollen. She gave a rational account of what she did this time, and it was consistent with what happened the first time. So why not give her the benefit of the doubt?"

Slowly, Ewen crossed out the names, leaving only *"Father; unknown."*

"That's all we can say for sure," he said at last, "I'll leave it at that."

In the large building which still served as refectory, kitchen and recreation hall—although a separate group-kitchen was going up, built of the heavy pale translucent native stone—a group of women from the New Hebrides Commune, in their tartan skirts and the warm uniform coats they wore with them now, were preparing dinner. One of them, a girl with long red hair, was singing in a light soprano voice:

> When the day wears away,
> Sad I wander by the water,
> Where a man, born of sun,
> Wooed the fairy's daughter,
> Why should I sit and sigh,
> Pulling bracken, pulling bracken
> All alone and weary?

She broke off as Judy came in:

"Dr. Lovat, everything's ready, I told them you were over at the hospital. So we went ahead without you."

"Thank you, Fiona. Tell me, what was that you were singing?"

"Oh, one of our island songs," Fiona said. "You don't speak Gaelic? I thought not—well, it's called the *Fairy's Love Song*—about a fairy who fell in love with a mortal man, and wanders the hills of Skye forever, still looking for him, wondering why he never came back to her. It's prettier in Gaelic."

"Sing it in Gaelic, then," Judy said, "it would be fearfully dull if only one language survived here! Fiona, tell me, the Father doesn't come to meals in the common room, does he?"

"No, someone takes it out to him."

"Can I take it out today? I'd like to talk to him," Judy said, and Fiona checked a rough work-schedule posted on the wall. "I wonder if we'll ever get permanent work-assignments until we know who's pregnant and who isn't? All right, I'll tell Elsie you've got it. It's one of those sacks over there."

She found Father Valentine toiling away in the grave-yard, surrounded by the great stones he was heaving into place in the monument. He took the food from her and unwrapped it, laying it out on a flat stone. She sat down beside him and said quietly, "Father, I need your help. I don't suppose you'd hear my confession?"

He shook his head slowly. "I'm not a priest any more, Dr. Lovat. How in the name of anything holy can I have the insolence to pass judgment in the name of God on someone else's sins?" He smiled faintly. He was a small slight man, no older than thirty, but now he looked haggard and old. "In any case, I've had a lot of time to think, heaving rocks out here. How can I honestly preach or teach the Gospel of Christ on a world where He never set foot? If God wants this world saved he'll have to send someone to save it . . . whatever that means." He put a spoon into the bowl of meat and grain. "You brought your own lunch? Good. In theory I accept isolation. In practice I find I crave the company of my fellow man much more than I ever thought I would."

His words dismissed the question of religion, but Judy, in her inner turmoil, could not let it drop so easily. "Then you're just leaving us without pastoral help of any sort, Father?"

"I don't think I ever did much in that line," Father Valentine said. "I wonder if any priest ever did? It goes without saying that anything I can do for anyone as a friend, I'll do—it's the least I can do; if I spent my life at it, it wouldn't begin to balance out what I did, but it's better than sitting around in sackcloth and ashes mouthing penitential prayers."

The woman said, "I can understand that, I suppose. But do you really mean there's no room for faith, or religion, Father?"

He made a dismissing gesture. "I wish you wouldn't call me 'father'. Brother, if you want to. We've all got to be brothers and sisters in misfortune here. No, I didn't say that, Doctor Lovat—I don't know your Christian name—Judith? I didn't say that, Judith. Every human being needs belief in the goodness of some power that created him, no matter what he calls it, and some religious or ethical structure. But I don't think we need sacraments or priesthoods from a world that's only a memory, and won't even be that to our children and our children's children. Ethics, yes. Art, yes. Music, crafts, knowledge, humanity—yes. But not rituals which will quickly dwindle down into superstitions. And certainly not

125

a social code or a set of purely arbitrary behavioral attitudes which have nothing to do with the society we're in now."

"Yet you would have worked in the Church structure at the Coronis colony?"

"I suppose so. I hadn't really thought about it. I belong to the Order of Saint Christopher of Centaurus, which was organized to carry the Reformed Catholic Church to the stars, and I simply accepted it as a worthy cause. I never really thought about it—not serious, hard, deep thought. But out here on my rock pile I've had a lot of time to think." He smiled faintly. "No wonder they used to put criminals to breaking rocks, back on Earth. It keeps your hands busy and gives you all your time for thought."

Judy said slowly, "So you don't think behavioral ethics are absolute, then? There's nothing definite or divinely ordained about them here?"

"How can there be? Judith, you know what I did. If I hadn't been brought up with the idea that certain things were in themselves, and of their very nature, enough to send me straight to hell, then when I woke up after the Wind, I could have lived with it. I might have been ashamed, or upset, or even sick at my stomach, but I wouldn't have had the conviction, deep down in my mind, that none of us deserved to *live* after it. In the seminary there were no shades of right and wrong, just virtue and sin, and nothing in between. The murders didn't trouble me, in my madness, because I was taught in seminary that lewdness was a mortal sin for which I could go to hell, so how could murder be any worse? You can go to hell only once, and I was already damned. A rational ethic would have told me that whatever those poor crewmen, God rest them, and I, had done during that night of madness, it had harmed only our dignity and our sense of decency, if that mattered. It was miles away, galaxies away, from murder."

Judy said, "I'm no theologian, Fa—er—Valentine, but can anyone truly commit a mortal sin in a state of complete insanity?"

"Believe me, I've been through that one and out the other side. It doesn't help to know that if I'd been able to run to my own confessor and get his forgiveness for all the things I did in my madness—ugly things by some

126

standards, but essentially harmless—I might have been able to keep from killing those poor men. There has to be something wrong with a system that means you can take guilt on and off like an overcoat. As for madness— nothing can come out in madness that wasn't there already. What I really couldn't face, I begin to realize, wasn't just the knowledge that in madness I'd done some forbidden things with other men, it was the knowledge that I'd done them gladly and willingly, that I no longer believed they were very wrong, and that forever after, any time I saw those men, I'd remember the time when our minds were completely open to one another and we knew each other's minds and bodies and hearts in the most total love and sharing any human beings could know. I knew I could never hide it again, and so I took out my little pocket knife and started trying to hide from *myself.*" He smiled wryly, a terrible death's head grin. "Judith, Judith, forgive me, you came to ask me for help, you asked me to hear your confession, and you've ended up listening to mine."

She said very gently, "If you're right, we'll all have to be priests to each other, at least as far as listening to each other and giving what help we can." One phrase he had spoken seized on her, and she repeated it aloud. *"Our minds were open to one another . . . the most total love and sharing any human beings could know.* That seems to be what this world has done to us. In different degrees, yes—but to all of us in some way or other. That's what he said"—and slowly, searching for words, she told him about the alien, their first meeting in the wood, how he had sent for her during the Wind, and the strange things he had told her, without speech.

"He told me—our people's minds were like half-shut doors," she said. "Yet we understood each other, perhaps more so because there had been that—that total sharing. But no one believes me!" she finished with a cry of despair. "They believe I'm mad, or lying!"

"Does it matter so much what they believe?" the priest asked slowly. "By their disbelief you might even be shielding him. You told me he was afraid of us—of your people—and if his kind are gentle people, I'm not surprised. A telepathic race tuned in to us during the Ghost Wind would probably have decided we were a horrifyingly violent, frightening people, and they wouldn't have been entirely wrong, although there's another side to us. But if they once begin believing in your—what is Fiona's phrase?—your fairy lover, they might seek out his people, and the results might not be very good." He smiled faintly. "Our race has a bad reputation when we meet other cultures we consider inferior. If you care about your child's father, Judy, I'd let them go on disbelieving in him."

"Forever?"

"As long as necessary. This planet is already changing us," Valentine said, "maybe some day our children and his will find some way of coming together without catastrophe, but we'll have to wait and see."

Judy pulled at the chain around her neck and he said, "Didn't you used to wear a cross on that?"

"Yes, I took it off, forgive me."

"Why? It doesn't mean anything here. But what is this?"

It was a blue jewel, blazing, with small silvery patterns moving within. "He said—they used these things for the training of their children; that if I could master the jewel I could reach him—let him know it was well with me and the child."

"Let me see it," Valentine said, and reached for it, but she flinched and drew away.

"What—?"

"I can't explain it. I don't understand it. But when anyone else touches it, now, it—it *hurts,* as if it was part of *me,*" she said fumblingly. "Do you think I'm mad?"

The man shook his head. "What's madness?" he asked. "A jewel to enhance telepathy—perhaps it has some peculiar properties which resonate to the electrical signals sent off by the brain—telepathy can't just exist, it must have some natural phenomenal basis. Perhaps the jewel is attuned to whatever it is in your mind that makes you *you.* In any case, it exists, and—have you reached him with it?"

"It seems so sometimes," said Judy, fumbling for words. "It's like hearing someone's voice and knowing whose it is by the sound—no, it's not quite like that either, but it does happen. I feel—very briefly, but it's quite real—as if he were standing beside me, touching me, and then it fades again. A moment of reassurance, a moment of—of love, and then it's gone. And I have the strange feeling that it's only a beginning, that a day will come when I'll know other things about it—"

He watched while she tucked the jewel away inside her dress again. At last he said, "If I were you, I'd keep it a secret for a while. You said this planet's changing us all, but perhaps it isn't changing us *fast* enough. There are some of the scientists who would want to test this thing, to work at it, perhaps even to take it from you, experiment, destroy it to see how it works. Perhaps even interrogate and test you again and again, to see if you are lying or hallucinating. Keep it secret, Judith. Use it as he told you. A day may come when it will be important to know how it works—the way it is supposed to work, not the way the scientists might want to make it work."

He rose, shaking the crumbs of his meal off his lap. "It's back to the rock pile for me."

She stood on the tips of her toes and kissed his cheek. "Thank you," she said softly, "you've helped me a lot."

The man touched her face. "I'm glad," he said. "It's— a beginning. A long road back, but it's a beginning. Bless you, Judith."

He watched her walk away, and a curious near-blasphemous thought touched his mind, *how do I know God isn't sending a Child . . . a strange child, not quite man . . . here on this strange world?* He dismissed the thought, thinking *I'm mad*, but another thought made him cringe with mingled memory and dismay, *how do we know the Child I worshipped all these years was not some such strange alliance?*

"Ridiculous," he said aloud, and bent over his self-imposed penance again.

Chapter
FOURTEEN

"I never thought I'd find myself praying for bad weather," Camilla said. She closed the door of the small repaired dome where the computer was housed, joining

Harry Leicester inside. "I've been thinking. With what data we have about the length of the days, the inclination of the sun, and so forth, couldn't we find out the exact length of this planet's year?"

"That's elementary enough," Leicester said. "Write up your program and feed it through. Might tell us how long a summer to expect and how long a winter."

She moved to the console. Her pregnancy was beginning to show now, although she was still light and graceful. He said, "I managed to salvage almost all of the information about the matter-anti-matter drives. Some day —Moray told me the other day that from the steam engine to the stars is less than three hundred years. Some day our descendants will be able to return to Earth, Camilla."

She said, "That's assuming they'll want to," and sat down at her desk. He looked at her in mild question. "Do you doubt it?"

"I'm not doubting anything, I'm just not presuming to know what my great-great-great-great—oh hell, what my ninth-generation grandsons will want to be doing. After all, Earthmen lived for generations without even wanting to invent things which could easily have been invented any time after the first smelting of iron was managed. Do you honestly think Earth would have gone into space without population pressure and pollution? There are so many social factors too."

"And if Moray has his way our descendants will all be barbarians," Leicester said, "but as long as we have the computer and it's preserved, the knowledge will be *there*. There for them to use, whenever they feel the need."

"*If* it's preserved," she said with a shrug. "After the last few months I'm not sure anything we brought here is going to outlive this generation."

Consciously, with an effort, Leicester reminded himself, *she's pregnant and that's why they thought for years that women weren't fit to be scientists—pregnant women get notions.* He watched her making swift notations in the elaborate shorthand of the computer. "Why do you want to know the length of the year?"

What a stupid question, the girl thought, then remembered he was brought up on a space station, weather is nothing to him. She doubted if he even realized the relationship of weather and climate to crops and survival. She

130

said, explaining gently, "First, we want to estimate the growing season and find out when our harvests can come in. It's simpler than trial and error, and if we'd colonized in the ordinary way, someone would have observed this planet through several year cycles. Also, Fiona and Judy and—and the rest of us would like to know when our children will be born and what the climate's likely to be like. I'm not making my own baby clothes, but someone's got to make them—and know how much chill to allow for!"

"You're planning already?" he asked, curiously. "The odds are only one in two that you'll carry it to term and the same that it won't die."

"I don't know. Somehow I never doubted that mine would be one of the ones to live. Premonition, maybe; ESP," she said, thinking slowly as she spoke. "I had a feeling Ruth Fontana would miscarry, and she did."

He shuddered. "Not a pleasant gift to have."

"No, but I seem to be stuck with it," she said matter-of-factly, "and it seems to be helping Moray and the others with the crops. Not to mention the well Heather helped them dig. Evidently it's simply a revival of latent human potential and there's nothing weird about it. Anyhow, it seems we'll have to learn to live with it."

"When I was a student," Leicester said, "all the facts known positively about ESP were fed into a computer and the answer was that the probability was a thousand to one that there was no such thing . . . that the very few cases not totally and conclusively disproven were due to investigator error, not human ESP."

Camilla grinned and said, "That just goes to show you that a computer isn't God."

Captain Leicester watched the young woman stretch back and ease her cramped body. "Damn these bridge seats, they were never meant for use in full gravity conditions. I hope comfortable furniture gets put on a fair priority; Junior here doesn't approve of my sitting on hard seats these days."

Lord, how I love that girl, who'd have believed it at my age! To remind himself more forcefully of the gap, Leicester said sharply, "Are you planning to marry Mac-Aran, Camilla?"

"I don't think so," she said with the ghost of a smile. "We haven't been thinking in those terms. I love him—

we came so close during the first Wind, we've shared so much, we'll always be part of each other. I'm living with him, when he's here—which isn't very often—if that's what you really want to know. Mostly because he wants me so much, and when you've been that close to anyone, when you can—" she fumbled for words, "when you can feel how much he wants you, you can't turn your back on him, you can't leave him—hungry and unhappy. But whether or not we can make any kind of home together, whether we want to live together for the rest of our lives—I honestly don't know; I don't think so. We're too different." She gave him a straightforward smile that made the man's heart turn over and said, "I'd really be happier with you, on a long-term basis. We're so much more alike. Rafe's so gentle, so sweet, but you understand me better."

"You're carrying his child, and you can say this to me, Camilla?"

"Does it shock you?" she asked, grieved, "I'm sorry, I wouldn't upset you for the world. Yes, it's Rafe's baby, and I'm glad, in a funny way. *He* wants it, and one parent *ought* to want a child; for me—I can't help it, I was brainwashed—it's still an accident of biology. If it was yours, for instance—and it could have been, the same kind of accident, just as Fiona's having *your* child and you hardly know her by sight—you'd have hated it, you'd have wanted me to fight against having it."

"I'm not so sure. Maybe not. Not now, anyhow," Harry Leicester said in a low voice. "Saying these things still upsets me, though. Shocks me. I'm too old, maybe."

She shook her head. "We've got to learn not to hide from each other. In a society where our children will grow up knowing that what they feel is an open book, what good is it going to be to keep sets of masks to wear from each other?"

"Frightening."

"A little. But they'll probably take it for granted." She leaned a little against him, easing her back against his chest. She reached back and took his fingers in hers. She said slowly, "Don't be shocked at this. But—if I live—if we both live—I'd like my next child to be yours."

He bent and kissed her on the forehead. He was almost too much moved to speak. She tightened her hand on his, then drew it away.

"I told MacAran this," she said matter-of-factly. "For genetic reasons, it's going to be a good thing for women to have children by different fathers. But—as I said—my reasons aren't quite as cold and unemotional as all that."

Her face took on a distant look—for a moment it seemed to Leicester that she was looking at something invisible through a veil—and for a moment contracted in pain; but to his quick, concerned question, she summoned a smile.

"No, I'm all right. Let's see what we can do about this year-length thing. Who knows, it might turn out to be our first National Holiday!"

The windmills were visible several miles from the Base Camp now, huge wooden-sailed constructs which supplied power for grinding flour and grain (nuts, harvested in the forest, made a fine slightly-sweet flour which would serve until the first crops of rye and oats were harvested) and also brought small trickles of electric power into the camp. But such power would always be in short supply on this world, and it was carefully rationed; for lights in the hospital, to operate essential machinery in the small metal shops and the new glass-house. Beyond the camp, with its own firebreak, was what they had begun to call New Camp, although the Hebrides Commune people who worked there called it New Skye; an experimental farm where Lewis MacLeod, and a group of assistants, were checking possibly domesticable animals.

Rafe MacAran, with his own small crew of assistants, paused to look back from the peak of the nearest hill before setting off into the forest. The two camps could both clearly be seen, from here, and around them both was swarming activity, but there was some indefinable difference from any camp he had seen on Earth, and for a moment he could not put his finger on it. Then he knew what it was; it was the quiet. Or was it? There was really plenty of sound. The great windmills creaked and heaved in the strong wind. There were crisp distant sounds of hammerings and sawings where the building crews were constructing winter buildings. The farm had its noises, including the noisy sounds of animals, the bellowings of the antlered mammals, the curious grunts, chirps, squeaks of unfamiliar life forms. And finally Rafe put his finger on it. There were no sounds which were not of natural origin.

133

No traffic. No machinery, except the softly whirring potter's wheels and the clinkings of tools. Each one of these sounds had some immediate human deliberation behind it. There were almost no impersonal sounds. Every sound seemed to have a purpose, and it seemed strange and lonesome to Rafe. All his life he had lived in the great cities of Earth, where even in the mountains, the sounds of all-terrain vehicles, motorized transit, high-tension power lines, and jet planes overhead, provided a comforting background. Here it was quiet, frighteningly quiet because whenever a sound broke the stillness of wind, there was some immediate *meaning* to the sound. You couldn't tune it out. Whenever there was a sound, you *had* to listen to it. There were no sounds which could be carelessly disregarded because, like jets passing overhead or the drive of the starship, you knew they had nothing to do with you. Every sound in the landscape had some immediate application to the listener, and Rafe felt tense most of the time, listening.

Oh well. He supposed he'd get used to it.

He started instructing his group. "We'll work along the lower rock-ridges today, and especially in the stream-beds. We want samples of every new-looking kind of earth —oh hell—*soil*. Every time the color of the clay or loam changes, take a sample of it, and locate it on the map— you're doing the mapping, Janice?" he asked the girl, and she nodded. "I'm working on grid paper. We'll get a location for every change of terrain."

The morning's work was relatively uneventful, except for one discovery near a stream-bed, which Rafe mentioned when they gathered to kindle a fire and make their noon-day meal—nut-flour rolls to be toasted and "tea" of a local leaf which had a pleasant, sweet taste like sassafras. The fire was kindled in a quickly-piled rock fireplace— the colony's strongest law was never to build a fire on the ground without firebreaks or rock enclosures—and as the quick resinous wood began to burn down to coals, a second small party came down the slope toward them: three men, two women.

"Hello, can we join you for dinner? It'll save building another fire," Judy Lovat greeted them.

"Glad to have you," MacAran agreed, "but what are you doing in the woods, Judy? I thought you were exempt from manual work now."

The woman gestured. "As a matter of fact, I'm being treated like surplus luggage," she said. "I'm not allowed to lift a finger, or do any real climbing, but it minimizes bringing samples back to camp if I can do preliminary field-testing on various plants. That's how we discovered the ropeweed. Ewen says the exercise will do me good, if I'm careful not to get overtired or chilled." She brought her tea and sat down beside him. "Any luck today?"

He nodded. "About time. For the last three weeks, every day, everything I brought in was just one more version of quartzite or calcite," he said. "Our last strike was graphite."

"Graphite? What good is that?"

"Well, among other things, it's the lead in a pencil," MacAran said, "and we have plenty of wood for pencils, which will help when supplies run low of other writing instruments. It can also be used to lubricate machinery, which will conserve supplies of animal and vegetable fats for food purposes."

"It's funny, you never think of things like that," Judy said. "The *millions* of little things you need that you always took for granted."

"Yes," said one of MacAran's crew. "I always thought of cosmetics as something extra—something people could do without in an emergency. Marcia Cameron told me the other day that she was working on a high-priority program for face cream, and when I asked why, she reminded me that in a planet with all this much snow and ice, it was an urgent necessity to keep the skin soft and prevent chapping and infections."

Judy laughed. "Yes, and right now we're going mad trying to find a substitute for cornstarch to make baby powder with. Adults can use talc, and there's plenty of that around, but if babies breathe the stuff they can get lung troubles. All the local grains and nuts won't grind fine enough; the flour is fine to eat but not absorbent enough for delicate little baby bottoms."

MacAran asked, "Just how urgent is that now, Judy?"

Judy shrugged. "On Earth, I'd have about two-and-a-half months to go. Camilla and I, and Alastair's girl Alanna, are running about neck-and-neck; the next batch is due about a month after that. Here—well, it's anybody's guess." She added, quietly, "We expect the winter will set

135

in before that. But you were going to tell me about what you found today."

"Fuller's earth," MacAran said, "or something so like it I can't tell the difference." At her blank look he elucidated, "It's used in making cloth. We get small supplies of animal fiber, something like wool, from the rabbit-horns, and they're plentiful and can be raised in quantity on the farm, but fuller's earth will make the cloth easier to handle and shrink."

Janice said, "You never think of asking a geologist for something to make *cloth*, for goodness' sake."

Judy said, "When you come down to it, every science is inter-related, although on Earth everything was so specialized we lost sight of it." She drank the last of her tea. "Are you heading back to Base Camp, Rafe?"

He shook his head. "No, it's into the woods for us, probably back in the hills where we went that first time. There may be streams which rise in the far hills and we're going to check them out. That's why Dr. Frazer is with us—he wants to find further traces of the people we sighted last trip, get some more accurate idea of their cultural level. We know they build bridges from tree to tree—we haven't tried to climb in them, they're evidently a lot lighter than we are and we don't want to break their artifacts or frighten them."

Judy nodded. "I wish I were going," she said, rather wistfully, "but I'm under orders never to be more than a few hours from Base Camp until after the baby is born." MacAran caught a look of deep longing in her eyes and, with that new ability to pick up emotions, reached out for her and said gently, "Don't worry, Judy. We won't trouble anyone we find, whether the little people who build the bridges, or—anyone else. If any of the beings here were hostile to us, we'd have found it out by now. We've no intention of bothering them. One of our reasons for going is to make sure we won't inadvertently infringe on their living space, or disturb anything they need for *their* survival. Once we know where *they're* settled, we'll know where we ought *not* to settle."

She smiled. "Thank you, Rafe," she said, softly. "That's good to know. If we're thinking along those lines, I guess I needn't worry."

Shortly after the two groups separated, the food-test-

136

ing crew working back toward Base Camp, while Mac-Aran's crew moved further into the deep hills.

Twice in the next ten-day period they saw minor traces of the small furred aliens with the big eyes; once, over a mountain watercourse, a bridge constructed of long linked and woven loops of reed, carefully twined together and fastened, with rope ladders leading up toward it from the lower levels of the trees. Without touching it, Dr. Frazer examined the vines of which it was constructed, saying that the need for fiber, rope and heavy twines were likely to be greater than the small supplies of what they called ropeweed could provide. Almost a hundred miles further into the hills, they found what looked like a ring of trees planted in a perfect circle, with more of the rope ladders leading up into the trees; but the place looked deserted and the platform which seemed to have been built across between the trees, of something like wickerwork, was dilapidated and the sky could be seen through wormholes in the bottom.

Frazier looked covetously upward. "I'd give five years off my life to get a look up there. Do they use furniture? Is it a house, a temple, who knows what? But I can't climb those trees and the rope ladders probably wouldn't even hold Janice's weight, let alone mine. As I remember, none of them were much bigger than a ten-year-old child."

"There's plenty of time," MacAran said. "The place is deserted, we can come back some day with ladders and explore to your heart's content. Personally I think it's a farm."

"A farm?"

MacAran pointed. On the regularly spaced treetrunks were extraordinarily straight lines; the delicious grey fungus which MacLeod had discovered before the first of the Winds was growing there in rows as neatly spaced as if they had been drawn on with a ruler. "They could hardly grow as neatly as this," MacAran said, "they must have been planted here. Maybe they come back every few months to harvest their crop, and the platform up there could be anything—a resthouse, a storage granary, an overnight camp. Or of course this could be a farm they abandoned years ago."

"It's nice to know the stuff can be cultivated," Frazer said, and began carefully making notes in his notebook

137

about the exact kind of tree on which it was growing, the spacing and height of the rows. "Look at this! It looks for all the world like a simple irrigation system, to divert water *away* from where the fungus is growing and directly to the roots of the tree!"

As they went on into the hills, the location of the alien "farm" firmly fixed on Janice's map, MacAran found himself thinking about the aliens. Primitive, yes, but what other type of society was seriously possible on this world? Their intelligence level must be comparable to that of many men, judging by the sophistication of their devices.

The Captain talks about a return to savagery. But I suspect we couldn't return if we tried. In the first place we're a selected group, half of us educated at the upper levels, the rest having been through the screening process for the Colonies. We come with knowledge acquired over millions of years of evolution and a few hundred years of forced technology pressured by an over-populated, polluted world. We may not be able to transplant our culture whole, this planet wouldn't survive it, and it would probably be suicide to try. But he doesn't have to worry about dropping back to a primitive level. Whatever we finally do with this world, the end result, I suspect, won't at least be below what we had on Earth, in terms of the human mind making the best use of what it finds. It will be different . . . probably in a few generations even I couldn't relate it to Earth culture. But humans can't be less than human, and intelligence doesn't function below its own level.

These small aliens had developed according to the needs of this world; a forest people, wearing fur (MacAran, shivering in the icy rain of a summer night, wished he had it) and living in symbiosis with the forests. But as nearly as he could judge their constructs were indicative of a high level of elegance and adaptiveness.

What had Judy called them? *The little brothers who are not wise.* And what about the *other* aliens? This planet had evidently brought forth *two* wholly sapient races, and they must co-exist to some degree. It was a good sign for humanity and the others. But Judy's alien —it was the only name he had and even now he found himself doubting the very existence of the others—must be near enough to human to father a child on an Earth-woman, and the thought was strangely disturbing.

On the fourteenth day of their journey they reached the lower slopes of the great glacier which Camilla had christened *The Wall Around the World*. It soared above them cutting off half the sky, and MacAran knew that even at this oxygen level it was unclimbable. There was nothing beyond these slopes except bare ice and rock, buffeted by the eternal icy winds, and nothing was to be gained by going on. But even as MacAran's party turned their back on the enormous mountain mass, his mind rejected that *unclimbable*. He thought, *no, nothing is impossible*. We can't climb it now. Perhaps not in my lifetime; certainly not for ten, twenty years. But it's not in human nature to accept limits like this. Some day either I'll come back and climb it, or my children will. Or *their* children.

"So that's as far as we go in one direction," Dr. Frazer said. "Next expedition had better go in the other direction. This way it's all forest, and more forest."

"Well, we can make use of the forests," MacAran said. "Maybe the other direction there's a desert. Or an ocean. Or for all we know, fertile valleys and even cities. Only time will tell."

He checked the maps they had been making, looking with satisfaction on the filled-in parts, but realizing that there was a lifetime to go. They camped that night at the very foot of the glacier, and MacAran woke up before dawn, perhaps wakened by the cessation of the soft thick nightly snow. He went out and looked at the dark sky and the unfamiliar stars, three of the four moons hanging like jewelled pendants below the high ridge of the mountain above, then his eyes and thoughts went back to the valley. His people were there, and Camilla, carrying his child. Far to the east was a dim glow where the great red sun would rise. MacAran was suddenly overcome with a great and unspeakable content.

He had never been happy on Earth. The Colony would have been better, but even there, he would have fitted into a world designed by other men, and not all his kind of men. Here he could have a share in the original design of things, carve out and create what he wanted for himself and his children to come and their children's children. Tragedy and castastrophe had brought them here, madness and death had ravaged them, and yet MacAran knew that he was one of the lucky ones. He had found his own place, and it was good.

It took them much of that day and the next to retrace their steps from the foot of the glacier, through sullen grey weather and heavy gathering cloud, and MacAran, who had begun to mistrust fine weather on this planet, nevertheless felt the now-familiar prickle of disquiet. Toward evening of the second day the snow began, heavy and harder than anything he had yet seen on this world. Even in their warm clothes the Earthmen were freezing, and their sense of direction was quickly lost in the world which had turned to a white whirling insanity without color, form or place. They dared not stop and yet it soon became obvious that they could not go on much longer through the deepening layers of soft powdery snow, through which they floundered, clinging to one another. They could only keep going *down*. Other directions no longer had meaning. Under the trees it was a little better, but the howling wind from the heights above them, the creaking and heaving of branch after branch like wind in the gigantic rigging of some sailing ship immense beyond imagining, filled the twilight with uncanny voices. Once, trying to shelter beneath a tree, they attempted to set up their tent, but the gale made it flap wildly and twice it was lost and they had to chase the blowing fabric through the snow until it became entangled around a tree and they could, after a fashion, reclaim it. But it was useless to them as shelter, and they grew colder and colder, their coats keeping them dry indeed, but doing almost nothing against the piercing cold.

Frazer muttered with chattering teeth, as they held on to one another in the lee of a larger tree than usual, "If it's like this in the summer, what the hell kind of storms are we going to have in the winter?"

MacAran said grimly, "I suspect, in the winter, none of us had better set foot outside the Base Camp." He thought of the storm after the first of the Winds, when he had searched for Camilla through the light snow. It had seemed like a blizzard to him then. How little he had known this world! He was overcome with poignant fear and a sense of regret. *Camilla. She's safe in the settlement, but will we ever get back there, will any of us?* He thought with a painful twinge of self-pity that he would

140

never see his child's face, then angrily dismissed the thought. They needn't give up and lie down to die yet, but there had to be some shelter somewhere. Otherwise they wouldn't outlast the night. The tent was no more good to them than a piece of paper, but there had to be a way.

Think. You were boasting to yourself about what a selected, intelligent group we were. Use it, or you might as well be an Australian bushman.

You might better. Survival is something they're damn good at. But you've been pampered all your life.

Survive, damn you.

He gripped Janice by one arm, Dr. Frazer by the other; reached past him to young Domenick, the boy from the Commune who had been studying geology for work in the Colony. He drew them all close together, and spoke over the howling of the storm.

"Can anyone see where the trees are thickest? Since there's not likely to be a cave here, or any shelter, we've got to do the best we can with underbrush, or anything to break the wind and keep dry."

Janice said, her small voice almost inaudible, "It's hard to see, but I had the impression there's something dark over there. If it isn't solid, the trees must be so thick I can't see through them. Is that what you mean?"

MacAran had had the same impression himself; now, with it confirmed, he decided to trust it. *He'd been led straight to Camilla, that other time.*

Psychic? Maybe so. What did he have to lose?

"Everyone hold hands," he directed, more in gesture than words, "If we lose each other we'll never find each other again." Gripping one another tightly, they began to struggle toward the place that was only a darker darkness against the trees.

Dr. Frazer's grip tightened hard on his arm. He put his face close to MacAran's and shouted, "Maybe I'm losing my mind, but I saw a *light*."

MacAran had thought it was afterimages spinning behind his wind-buffeted eyes. What he thought he saw beyond it was even more unlikely; the figure of a man? Tall and palely shining and naked even in the storm—no, it was gone, it had been only a vision, but he thought the creature had beckoned from the dark loom . . . they struggled toward it. Janice muttered, "Did you see it?"

"Thought I did."

Afterward, when they were in the shelter of the thickly laced trees, they compared notes. No two of them had seen the same thing. Dr. Frazer had seen only the light. MacAran had seen a naked man, beckoning. Janice had seen only a face with a curious light around it, as if the face—she said—were really inside her own head, vanishing like the Cheshire cat when she narrowed her eyes to see it better; and to Domenick it had been a figure, tall and shining—"Like an angel," he said, "or a woman—a woman with long shining hair." But, stumbling after it, they had come against trees so thickly grown that they could hardly force their way between them; MacAran dropped to the ground and wriggled through, dragging them after.

Inside the clump of thickly growing trees the snow was only a light spray, and the howling wind could not reach them. They huddled together, wrapped in blankets from their packs and sharing body warmth, nibbling at rations cold from their dinner. Later, MacAran struck a light, and saw, against the bole of the tree, carefully fastened flat pieces of wood. A ladder, against the side of the tree, leading upwards. . . .

Even before they began climbing he guessed that this was not one of the houses of the small furred folk. The rungs were far enough apart to give even MacAran some trouble and Janice, who was small, had to be pulled up them. Dr. Frazer demurred, but MacAran never hesitated.

"If we all saw something different," he said, "we were *led* here. *Something* spoke directly to our minds. You might say we were *invited*. If the creature was naked—and two of us saw him, or it, that way—evidently the weather doesn't bother them, whatever they are, but it knows that we're in danger from it. I suggest we accept the invitation, with a proper respect."

They had to wriggle through a loosely tied door up through on to a platform, but then they found themselves inside a tightly-built wooden house. MacAran started to strike his light carefully again, and discovered that it was not necessary, for there was indeed a dim light inside, coming from some kind of softly glowing, phosphorescent stuff against the walls. Outside the wind wailed and the boughs of the great trees creaked and swayed, so that the soft floor of the dwelling had a slight motion, not unpleasant but a little disquieting. There was a single large room; the floor was covered with something soft and spongy, as if moss or some soft winter grass grew there of itself. The exhausted, chilled travellers stretched out gratefully, relaxing in the comparative warmth, dryness, shelter, and slept.

Before MacAran slept it seemed to him that in the distance he heard a high sweet sound, like singing, through the storm. Singing? Nothing could live out there, in this blizzard! Yet the impression persisted, and at the very edge of sleep, words and pictures persisted in his mind.

Far below in the hills, astray and maddened after his first exposure to the Ghost Wind, coming back to sanity to discover the tent carefully set up and their packs and scientific equipment neatly piled inside. Camilla thought he had done it. He had thought *she* had done it.

Someone's been watching us. Guarding us.

Judy was telling the truth.

For an instant a calm beautiful face, neither male nor female, swam in his mind. "Yes. We know you are here. We mean you no harm, but our ways lie apart. Nevertheless we will help you as we can, even though we can only reach you a little, through the closed doors of your minds. It is better if we do not come too close; but sleep tonight in safety and depart in peace. . . ."

In his mind there was a light around the beautiful features, the silver eyes, and neither then nor ever did MacAran ever know whether he had seen the eyes of the alien or the lighted features, or whether his mind had received them and formed a picture made up of childhood dreams of angels, of fairy-folk, of haloed saints. But to the sound of the faraway singing, and the lulling noise of the wind, he slept.

Chapter
FIFTEEN

". . . and that was really all there was to it. We stayed inside for about thirty-six hours, until the snow ended

143

and the wind quieted, then we went away again. We never had a glimpse of whoever lived there; I suspect he carefully kept away until we were gone. It wasn't there that he took you, Judy?"

"Oh, no. Not so far. Not nearly. And it wasn't to any home of his own people. It was, I think, one of the cities of the little people, the men of the tree-roads, he called them, but I couldn't find the place again, I wouldn't want to," she said.

"But they have good will toward us, I'm sure of that," MacAran said, "I suppose—it wasn't the same one you knew?"

"How can I possibly know? But they're evidently a telepathic race; I suspect anything known to one of them is known to others—at least to his intimates, his family—if they have families."

MacAran said, "Perhaps, some day, they'll know we mean them no harm."

Judy smiled faintly and said, "I'm sure they know that you—and I—mean them no harm; but there are some of us they don't know, and I suspect that perhaps time doesn't matter to them as much as it does to us. That's not even so alien, except to us Western Europeans—Orientals even on Earth often made plans and thought in terms of generations instead of months or even years. Possibly he thinks there's time to get to know us any century now."

MacAran chuckled. "Well, we're not going anyplace. I guess there's time enough. Dr. Frazer is in seventh heaven, he's got anthropological notes enough to provide him with a spare-time job for three years. He must have written down everything he saw in the house—I hope they're not offended by his looking at everything. And of course he made notes of everything used as food—if we're anywhere near the same species, anything they can eat we can evidently eat," MacAran added. "We didn't touch his supplies, of course, but Frazer made notes of everything he had. I say he for convenience, Domenick was sure it was a woman who had led us there. Also the one piece of furniture—major furniture—was what looked like a loom, with a web strung on it. There were pods of some sort of vegetable fiber—it looked something like milkweed on Earth—soaking, evidently to prepare them for spinning into thread; we found some pods like it on

144

the way back and turned them over to MacLeod on the farm, they seem to make a very fine cloth."

Judy said, as he rose to go, "You realize there are still plenty of people in the camp who don't even believe there are any alien peoples on this planet."

MacAran met her lost eyes and said very gently, "Does it matter, Judy? We know. Maybe we'll just have to wait, and start thinking in terms of generations, too. Maybe our children will all know."

On the world of the red sun, the summer moved on. The sun climbed daily a little higher in the sky, a solstice was passed, and it began to angle a little lower; Camilla, who had set herself a task of keeping calendar charts, noted that the daily changes in sun and sky indicated that the days, lengthening for their first four months on this world, were shortening again toward the unimaginable winter. The computer, given all the information they had, had predicted days of darkness, mean temperatures in the level of zero centigrade, and virtually constant glacial storms. But she reminded herself that this was only a mathematical projection of probabilities. It had nothing to do with actualities.

There were times, during that second third of her pregnancy, when she wondered at herself. Never before this had it occurred to her to doubt that the severe discipline of mathematics and science, her world since childhood, had any lacunae; or that she would ever come up against any problem, except for strictly personal ones, which these disciplines could not solve. As far as she could tell, the old disciplines still held good for her crewmates. Even the growing evidence of her own increasing ability to read the minds of others, and to look uncannily into the future and make unsettlingly accurate guesses based only on quick flashes of what she had to call "hunch" —even this was laughed at, shrugged aside. Yet she knew that some of the others experienced much the same thing.

It was Harry Leicester—she still secretly thought of him as Captain Leicester—who put it most clearly for her, and when she was with him she could see it almost as he did.

"Hold on to what you *know*, Camilla. That's all you can do; it's known as intellectual integrity. If a thing is impossible, it's *impossible*."

145

"And if the impossible happens? Like ESP?"

"Then," he said hardily, "you have somehow misinterpreted your facts, or are making guesses based on subliminal cues. Don't go overboard on this because of your will to believe. Wait for *facts*."

She asked him quietly, "Just what would you consider evidence?"

He shook his head. "Quite frankly, there is *nothing* I would consider evidence. If it happened to me, I should simply certify myself as insane and the experience of my senses therefore worthless."

She thought then, *what about the will to disbelieve? And how can you have intellectual integrity when you throw out one whole set of facts as impossible before you even test them?* But she loved the Captain and the old habits held. Some day, perhaps, there would be a showdown, but she hoped, with a quiet desperation, that it would not come soon.

The nightly rain continued, and there were no more of the frightening winds of madness, but the tragic statistics which Ewen Ross had foreseen went on, with a fearful inevitability. Of one hundred and fourteen women, some eighty or ninety should, within five months, have become pregnant; forty-eight actually did so, and of these, twenty-two miscarried within two months. Camilla knew she was going to be one of the lucky ones, and she was; her pregnancy went on so uneventfully that there were times when she completely forgot about it. Judy, too, had an uneventful pregnancy; but the girl from the Hebrides Commune, Alanna, went into labor in the sixth month and gave birth to premature twins who died within seconds of delivery. Camilla had little contact with the girls of the Commune—most of them were working at New Skye, except for the pregnant ones in the hospital—but when she heard that, something went through her that was like pain, and she sought out MacAran that night and stayed with him a long time, clinging to him in a wordless agony she could neither explain nor understand. At last she said, "Rafe, do you know a girl named Fiona?"

"Yes, fairly well; a beautiful redhead in New Skye. But you needn't be jealous, darling, as a matter of fact, I think she's living with Lewis MacLeod just now. Why?"

"You know a lot of people in New Skye. Don't you?"

"Yes, I've been there a lot lately, why? I thought you

had them down for disgusting savages," Rafe said, a little defensively, "but they're nice people and I like their way of life. I'm not asking you to join them. I know you wouldn't, and they won't let me in without a woman of my own—they try to keep the sexes balanced, though they don't marry—but they treat me like one of them."

She said with unusual gentleness, "I'm very glad, and I'm certainly not jealous. But I'd like to see Fiona, and I can't explain why. Could you take me to one of their meetings?"

"You don't have to explain," he said, "They're having a concert—oh, informal, but that's what it is—tonight, and anyone who wants to come is welcome. You could even join in, if you felt like singing, I do sometimes. You know some old Spanish songs, don't you? There's a sort of informal project to preserve as much music as we can remember."

"Some other time, I'll be glad to; I'm too short of breath to do much singing now," she said. "Maybe after the baby's born." She clasped his hand, and MacAran felt a wild pang of jealousy. *She knows Fiona's carrying the Captain's child, and she wants to see her. And that's why she isn't jealous, she couldn't care less. . . .*

I'm jealous. But would I want her to lie to me? She does love me, she's having my child, what more do I want?

They heard the music beginning before they reached the new Community Hall at the New Skye farm, and Camilla looked at MacAran in startled dismay. "Good Lord, what's that unholy racket!"

"I forgot you weren't a Scot, darling, don't you like the bagpipes? Moray and Domenick and a couple of others play them, but you don't have to go in until they're finished unless you like," he laughed.

"It sounds worse than a banshee on the loose," Camilla said firmly. "The music isn't all like that, I hope?"

"No, there are harps, guitars, lutes, you name it, they've got it. And building new ones." He squeezed her fingers as the pipes died, and they walked toward the hall. "It's a tradition, that's all. The pipes. And the Highland regalia —the kilts and swords."

Camilla felt, surprisingly, a brief pang almost of envy as they came into the hall, brightly lit with candles and torches; the girls in their brilliant tartan skirts and plaids, the men resplendent in kilts, swords, buckled plaids swaggering over their shoulders. So many of them were bright-haired redheads. *A colorful tradition. They pass it on, and our traditions—die. Oh, come, damn it, what traditions? The annual parade of the Space Academy? Theirs fit, at least, into this strange world.*

Two men, Moray and the tall, red-headed Alastair, were doing a sword dance, leaping nimbly across the gleaming blades to the sound of the piper. For an instant Camilla had a strange vision of gleaming swords, not used in games, but deadly serious, then it flickered out again and she joined in the applause for the dancers.

There were other dances and songs, mostly unfamiliar to Camilla, with a strange, melancholy lilt and a rhythm that made her think of the sea. And the sea, too, ran through many of the words. It was dark in the hall, even by the torchlight, and she did not anywhere see the coppery-haired girl she sought, and after a time she forgot the urgency that had brought her there, listening to the mournful songs of a vanished world of islands and seas;

> O Mhari Oh, Mhari my girl
> Thy sea-blue eyes with witchery
> Draw me to thee, off Mull's wild shore
> My heart is sore, for love of thee. . . .

MacAran's arm tightened around her and she let herself lean against him.

She whispered, "How strange, that on a world without seas, so many sea-songs should be kept alive. . . ."

He murmured, "Give us time. We'll find some seas to sing about—" and broke off, for the song had died, and someone called, "Fiona! Fiona, you sing for us!" Others took up the cry, and after a time the slight red-haired girl, wearing a full green-and-blue skirt which accentuated, almost flaunting, her pregnancy, came through the crowd. She said, in her light sweet voice, "I can't do much singing, I'm short of breath these days. What would you like to hear?"

Someone called out in Gaelic; she smiled and shook her head, then took from another girl a small harp and sat on a wooden bench. Her fingers moved in soft arpeggios for a moment, and then she sang:

148

The wind from the island brings songs of our sorrow
The cry of the gulls and the sighing of streams;
In all of my dreaming, I'm hearing the waters
That flow from the hills in the land of our dreams.

Her voice was low and soft, and as she sang Camilla
caught the picture of green, low hills, familiar outlines of
childhood, memories of an Earth few of them could remember, kept alive only in songs such as this; memories
of a time when the hills of Earth were green beneath a
golden-yellow sun, and sea-blue skies. . . .

Blow westward, O sea-wind, and bring us some murmur
Adrift from our homeland of honour and truth;
In waking and sleeping, I'm hearing the waters
That flow from the hills in the land of our youth.

Camilla's throat tightened with half a sob. The lost
land, the forgotten . . . for the first time, she made a
clear effort to open the eyes of her mind to the special
awareness she had known since the first wind. She fixed
her eyes and her mind, almost fiercely, with a surge almost
of passionate love, on the singing girl; and then she saw,
and relaxed.

She won't die. Her child will live.

*I couldn't have borne it, for him to be wiped out as
if he'd never been . . .*

*What's wrong with me? He's only a few years older
than Moray, there's no reason he shouldn't outlive most
of us . . .* but the anguish was there, and the intense
relief, as Fiona's song swelled into a close;

We sing in this far land the songs of our exile,
The pipes and the harps are as fair as before;
But never shall music run sweet as the waters
That flow in that land we shall never see more.

Camilla discovered that she was weeping; but she was
not alone. All around her, in the darkened room, the
exiles were mourning their lost world; unable to bear it,
Camilla rose and blindly made her way toward the door,
groping through the crowds. When they saw that she was
pregnant they courteously cleared a way for her. Mac-
Aran followed, but she took no notice of him; only when

149

they were outside, she turned to him and stood, clinging to him, weeping wildly. But when at last she began to hear his concerned questions, she turned them aside. She did not know how to answer.

Rafe tried to comfort her, but somehow he picked up her disquiet, and for some time he did not know why, until abruptly it came to him.

Overhead the night was clear, with no cloud or sign of rain. Two great moons, lime-green, peacock-blue, hung low in the darkening violet sky. And the winds were rising.

Inside the Hall of the New Hebrides Commune, music passed imperceptibly into an almost ecstatic group dance, the growing sense of togetherness, of love and communion binding them together into bonds of closeness which were never to be forgotten or broken. Once, late in the night when the torches were flaring and guttering low, two of the the men sprang up, facing one another in a flare-up of violent wrath, swords flickering from their flamboyant Highland regalia, crossing in a clash of steel. Moray, Alastair and Lewis MacLeod, acting like the fingers of a single hand, dived at the two angry men and brought them sprawling down, knocking the swords out of their hands, and sat on them—literally—until the gleam of wolfish anger died in the two. Then, gently freeing them they poured whisky down their throats (*Scots will somehow manage to make whisky at the far ends of the Universe,* Moray thought, *no matter what else they go without*) until the two fighting men embraced one another drunkenly and pledged eternal friendship and the love-feast went on, until the red sun rose, clear and cloudless in the sky.

Judy woke, feeling the stir of the wind like a breath of cold through her very bones, the waking strangeness in her brain and bones. She felt quickly, as if seeking to reassure herself, where her child stirred with a strange strong life. *Yes. It is well with her, but she too feels the winds of madness.*

It was dark in the room where she lay, and she listened to the sounds of distant song. *It is beginning, but this time . . . this time do they know what it is, can they meet it without fear or strangeness?* She herself felt perfect calm, a silence at her center of being. She knew, without surprise, exactly what had brought the madness at first; and knew that for her, at least, madness would not return. There would always, in the season of the winds, be strangeness, and a greater openness and awareness; the latent powers, so long dormant, would always be stronger under the influence of the powerful psychedelic borne on the wind. But she knew, now, how to cope with them, and there would be only the small madness which eases the mind and rests the unquiet brain from stress, leaving it free to cope with further stress another time. She let herself drift on it now, reaching out with her thoughts for a half-felt touch that was like a memory. She felt as if she were spinning, floating on the winds that tossed her thoughts, and briefly her thoughts clasped and linked with the alien (even now she had no name for him, she needed none, they knew each other as a mother knows the face of her child or as twin recognizes twin, they would be together always even if her living eyes never again beheld his face) in a brief, half-ecstatic joining. Brief as the touch was, she needed, desired no more.

She drew out the jewel, his love-gift. It seemed to her to glow in the darkness with its own inner fire, as it had glowed in his hand when he laid it in hers in the forest, echoing the strange silver blue glow of his eyes. *Try to master the jewel.* She focused her eyes and thoughts on it, struggling to know, with that curious inner sight, what was meant.

It was dark in her room, for as the night moved on the moons sank behind the shuttered window and the starlight was dim. The jewel still clasped in her hand, Judy reached for a resin-candle; sleep was far from her. She felt about in the darkness for a light, missed it and heard the small chemical-tipped splinter fall to the floor. She whispered a small irritable imprecation, now she would have to get out of bed and find it. She stared fiercely at the resin-candle, somehow looking *through* the jewel in her hand.

Light, damn you.

The resin-candle on its carven stick suddenly flared into brilliant flame, untouched. Judy, gasping and feeling her heart pound, quickly snuffed the flame, took her hand away; again centered all her thoughts on the jewel and the flame and saw the light flare out again between her fingers.

So this is what they were. . . .

This could be dangerous. I will hide it until the proper time comes. In that moment she knew she had made a discovery which might, one day, step into the gap between the transplanted knowledge of Earth and the old knowledge of this strange world, but she also knew that she would not speak of it for a long time, if ever. *When the time comes and their minds are strong and ready, then—then perhaps they can be trusted with it. If I show them now, half of them will not believe—and the rest will begin to scheme how to use it.* Not now.

Since the destruction of the starship and his acceptance that they were marooned on this world (*A lifetime? Forever? Forever for me, at least*) Captain Leicester had had only one hope, a lifework, something to give reason to his existence and some glimmer of optimism to his despair.

Moray could structure a society which would tie them to the soil of this world, rooting like hogs for their daily food. That was Moray's business; maybe it was necessary for the time being, to evolve a stable society which could insure survival. But survival didn't matter if it was *only* survival, and he now realized it could be more. It would some day take their children back to the stars. He had the computer; and he had a technically trained crew, and he had a lifetime of knowledge. For the last three months he had systematically, piece by piece, stripped the ship of every bit of equipment, every bit of his own training for a lifetime, and programmed, with the help of Camilla and three other technicians, everything he knew into it. He had read every surviving textbook from the library into it, from astronomy to zoology, from medicine to electronic engineering; he had brought in every surviving crew member, one by one, and helped them to transfer all their knowledge to the computer. Nothing was too small to program into the computer, from how to build and repair a food synthesizer, to the making and repair of zippers on uniforms.

He thought, in triumph; there's a whole technology here, a whole heritage, preserved entire for our descendants. It won't be in my lifetime, or Moray's, or perhaps in my children's lifetime. But when we grow past the small struggles of day-to-day survival, the knowledge will be there, the heritage. It will be here for now, whether the knowledge for the hospital of how to cure a brain tumor or glaze a cooking-pot for the kitchen; and when Moray runs up against problems in his structured society, as he inevitably will, the answers will be here. The whole history of the world we came from; we can pass by all the blind alleys of society, and go straight to a technology which will take us back to the stars one day—to rejoin the greater community of civilized man, not crawling around on one planet, but spreading like a great branching tree from star to star, universe upon universe.

We can all die, but the thing which made us human will survive—entire—and some day we will go back. Some day we will reclaim it.

He lay and listened to the distant sound of singing from the New Skye hall, in the dome which had become his whole life. Vaguely it occurred to him that he should get up; dress; go over to them, join them. *They had something to preserve too.* He thought of the lovely copperhaired girl he had known so briefly; who, amazingly, bore his child.

She would be glad to see him, and surely he had some responsibility, even though he had fathered the child halfknowing, maddened like a beast in rut—he flinched at the thought. Still she had been gentle and understanding, and he owed her something, some kindness for having used and forgotten her. What was her strange and lovely name? *Fiona?* Gaelic, surely. He rose from his bed, searching quickly for some garments, then hesitated, standing at the door of the dome and looking out at the clear bright sky. The moons had set and the pale false dawn was beginning to glow far to the east, a rainbow light like an aurora, which he supposed was reflected from the faraway glacier he had never seen; would never see; never cared to see.

He sniffed the wind and as he drew it into his lungs a strange, angry suspicion came over him. Last time they had destroyed the ship; this time they would destroy him, and his work. He slammed the dome and locked it; double-locked it with the padlock he had demanded from Moray. This time no one would approach the computer, not even those he trusted most. Not even Patrick. Not even Camilla.

"Lie still, beloved. Look, the moons have set, it will be morning soon," Rafe murmured. "How warm it is, under the stars in the wind. Why are you crying, Camilla?"

She smiled in the darkness. "I'm not crying," she said softly, "I'm thinking that some day we'll find an ocean—and islands—for the songs we heard tonight, and that some day our children will sing them there."

"Have you come to love this world as I do, Camilla?"

"Love? I don't know," she said tranquilly, "it's *our* world. We don't have to love it. We only have to learn to live with it, somehow. Not on our terms but on its own."

All across Base Camp, the minds of the Earthmen flickered into madness, unexplained joy or fear; women wept without knowing why, or laughed in sudden joy they could not explain. Father Valentine, asleep in his isolated shelter, woke and came quietly down the mountain, and unnoticed, came into the Hall in New Skye, mingling with them in love and complete acceptance. When the winds died he would return to solitude, but he knew he would never be wholly alone again.

Heather and Ewen, sharing the night duty in the hospital, watched the red sun rise in the cloudless sky. Arms enlaced, they were shaken out of their silent ecstatic watching of the sky (a thousand ruby sparkles, the brilliant rush of light driving back the darknesses) by a cry behind them; a shrill, moaning wail of pain and terror.

A girl rushed toward them from her bed, panicked at the sudden pain, the gushing blood; Ewen lifted her and laid her down, mustering his strength and calm, trying to focus sanity (*you can get on top of it! Fight! Try!*) but stopped in the very act, arrested by what he saw in her frightened eyes. Heather touched him compassionately.

"No," she said, "no need to try."

"Oh, God, Heather, I can't, not like that, I can't bear it—"

The girl's eyes were wide and terrified. "Can't you help me?" she begged. "Oh, help me, help me—"

Heather knelt and gathered the girl in her arms. "No, darling," she said gently. "No, we can't help you, you're going to die. Don't be afraid, Laura darling, it will be very quick, and we'll be with you. Don't cry, darling,

154

don't cry, there's nothing to be afraid of." She held the girl close in her arms, murmuring to her, comforting her, sensing every bit of fear and trying with the strength of their rapport to soothe her, until the girl lay quiet and peaceful on her shoulder. They held her like that, crying with her, until she stopped breathing; then they laid her gently on the bed, covered her with a sheet, and sorrowfully, hand in hand, walked out into the sunrise and wept for her.

Captain Harry Leicester saw the sun rise, rubbing weary eyes. He had not taken his eyes from the console of the computer, watching over the only hope to save this world from barbarism. Once, shortly before dawn, he had thought he heard Camilla's voice calling to him from the doorway, but it was surely delusion. (*Once she had shared his dream. What had happened?*)

Now, in a strange, uneasy half-doze, half-trance, he watched a procession through his mind of strange creatures, not quite men, lifting strange starships into the red sky of this world, and, centuries later, returning. (*What had they been seeking, in the world beyond the stars? Why had they not found it?*) Could the quest after all be endless or even come full circle and end in its beginning?

But we have something to build on, the history of a world.

Another world. Not this one.

Are the answers of another world fit for this one?

He told himself furiously that knowledge was knowledge, that knowledge was power, and could save them—

—or destroy. After the long struggle to survive, will they not seek old answers, ready-made from the past, and try to re-create the desperate history of Earth, here on a world with a more fragile chain of life? Suppose, one day, they come to believe, as I seemed to believe for a time, that the computer really does have all the answers?

Well, doesn't it?

He rose and went to the doorway of the dome. The shuttered window, made small against the bitter cold, and high, swung wide at his touch and he looked out at the sunrise and the strange sun. *Not mine. But theirs.* Someday they will unlock its secrets.

With my help. My single-handed struggle to keep for

155

them a heritage of true knowledge, a whole technology to take them back to the stars.

He breathed deep, and began to listen silently to the sounds of this world. The winds in the trees and the forests, the running of the streams, the beasts and birds that lived their own strange secret lives deep in the woods, the unknown aliens whom his descendants would one day know.

And they would not be barbarian. They would *know*. If they were tempted to explore some blind alley of knowledge, the answer would be there, ready for their asking, ready with its reply.

(Why did Camilla's voice echo in his mind? *"That only proves that a computer isn't God."*)

Isn't the truth a form of God? he demanded wildly of himself and of the universe. *Ye shall know the truth and the truth shall make you free.*

(Or enslave you? Can one truth hide another?)

Suddenly a horrid vision came into his mind, as his thoughts burst free from time and slid into the future, which lay quivering before him. A race taught to go for all its answers here, to the shrine which had all the *right* answers. A world where no question could ever be left open, for it had *all* the answers, and what lay outside it was not possible to explore.

A barbarian world with the computer worshipped as a God.

A God. A God. A God.

And he was creating that God.

God! Am I insane?

And the answer came, clear and cold. No. I have been insane since the ship crashed, but now I am sane. Moray was right all along. The answers of another world are not the answers we can use here. *The* technology, *the* science, are only a technology and a science for Earth, and if we try to transfer them here, whole, we will destroy this planet. Some day, not as soon as I would wish, but in their own good time, they will evolve a technology rooted in the soil, the stones, the sun, the resources of this world. Perhaps it will take them to the stars, if they want to go. Perhaps it will take them into time or the inner spaces of their own hearts. But it will be theirs, not mine. I am not a God. I cannot make a world in my own image.

He had brought all the supplies of the ship from the bridge to this dome. Now, quietly, he turned and began to fashion what he sought, old words from another world ringing in his mind;

Endless the world's turn, endless the sun's spinning
Endless the quest;
I turn again, back to my own beginning,
And here, find rest.

With steady hands he lighted a resin-candle and, deliberately, set a light to the long fuse.

Camilla and MacAran heard the explosion and ran toward the dome, just in time to see it erupt skyward in a shower of debris, and rising flame.

Fumbling with the padlock, Harry Leicester began to realize that he wasn't going to get out. This time he wasn't going to make it. Staggering from the blow and concussion, but coldly, gladly sane, he looked at the wreckage. *I've given you a clean start,* he thought confusedly, maybe I am God after all, the one who drove Adam and Eve out of Eden and stopped telling them all the answers, letting them find their own way, and grow . . . no lifelines, no cushions, let them find their own way, live or die. . . .

He hardly knew it when they forced the door open and took him up gently, but he felt Camilla's gentle touch on his dying mind and opened his eyes into the blue compassionate stare.

He whispered in confusion, *"I am a very foolish fond old man. . . ."*

Her tears fell on his face. "Don't try to talk. I know why you did it. We began to do it together, last time, and then . . . oh, Captain, Captain. . . ."

He closed his eyes. "Captain of *what?*" he whispered. And then, at his last breath, "You can't retire a Captain. You have to shoot him . . . and I shot him. . . ."

And then the red sun went out, forever, and blazed into luminous galaxies of light.

Epilogue

Even the struts of the starship were gone, carried away to the hoarded stores of metal; mining would always be slow on this world, and metals scarce for many, many generations. Camilla, from habit, gave the place a glance, but no more, as she went across the valley. She walked lightly, a tall woman, her hair lightly touched with frost, as she followed a half-heard awareness. Beyond the range of vision she saw the tall stone memorial to the crash victims, the graveyard where all the dead of the first terrible winter were buried beside the dead from the first summer and the winds of madness. She drew her fur cloak around her, looking with a regret so long past that it was no longer even sadness, at one of the green mounds.

MacAran, coming down the valley from the mountain road, saw her, wrapped in her furs and her tartan skirt, and raised his hand in greeting. His heart still quickened at the sight of her, after so many years; and when he reached her, he took both her hands for a moment and held them before he spoke.

She said, "The children are well—I visited Mhari this morning. And you, I can tell without asking that you had a good trip." Letting her hand rest in his, they turned back together through the streets of New Skye. Their household was at the very end of the street, where they could see the tall East Peak, beyond which the red sun rose every morning in cloud; at one end, the small building which was the weather station; Camilla's special responsibility.

As they came into the main room of the house they shared with half a dozen other families, MacAran threw off his fur jacket and went to the fire. Like most men in the colony who did not wear kilts, he wore leather breeches and a tunic of woven tartan cloth. "Is everyone else out?"

"Ewen is at the hospital; Judy is at the school; Mac

158

went off with the herding drive," she said, "and if you're dying for a look at the children I think they're all in the schoolyard but Alastair. He's with Heather this morning."

MacAran walked to the window, looking at the pitched roof of the school. How quickly they grew tall, he thought, and how lightly fourteen years of childbearing lay on their mother's shoulders. The seven who had survived the terrible famine winter five years ago were growing up. Somehow they had weathered, together, the early storms of this world; and although she had had children by Ewen, by Lewis MacLeod, by another whose name he had never known and he suspected Camilla herself did not know, her two oldest children and her two youngest were his. The last, Mhari, did not live with them; Heather had lost a child three days before Mhari's birth and Camilla, who had never cared to nurse her own children if there was a wet-nurse available, had given her to Heather to nurse; when Heather was unwilling to give her up after she was weaned, Camilla had agreed to let Heather keep her, although she visited her almost every day. Heather was one of the unlucky ones; she had borne seven children but only one had lived more than a month after birth. Ties of fosterage in the community were stronger than blood; a child's mother was only the one who cared for it, its father the one who taught it. MacAran had children by three other women, and cared for them all equally, but he loved best Judy's strange young Lori, taller than Judy at fourteen and yet childlike and peculiar, called a changeling by half the community, her unknown father still a secret to all but a few.

Camilla said, "Now you're back, when are you off again?"

He slid an arm around her. "I'll have a few days at home first, and then—we're off to find the sea. There *must* be one, somewhere on this world. But first—I have something for you. We explored a cave, a few days ago—and found these, in the rock. We don't have much use for jewels, I know, it's really a waste of time to dig them out, but Alastair and I liked the looks of these, so we brought some home to you and the girls. I had a sort of feeling about them."

From his pocket he took a handful of blue stones, pouring them into her hands, looking at the surprise and pleasure in her eyes. Then the children came running in, and MacAran found himself swamped in childish kisses, hugs, questions, demands.

"Da, can I go to the mountains with you next time? Harry goes and he's only fourteen!"

"Da, Alanna took my cakes, make her give them back!"

"Dada, Dada, look here, look here! See me climb!"

Camilla, as always, ignored the hullabaloo, calmly gesturing them to quiet. "One question at a time—what is it, Lori?"

The silver-haired child with grey eyes picked up one of the blue stones, looking at the starlike patterns coiled within. She said gravely, "My mother has one like this. May I have one, too? I think perhaps I can work it as she does."

MacAran said, "You may have one," and over her head looked at Camilla. Some day, in Lori's own time, they would know exactly what she meant, for their strange fosterling never did anything without reason.

"You know," Camilla said, "I think some day these are going to be very, very important to all of us."

MacAran nodded. Her intuition had been proven right so many times that now he expected it; but he could wait. He walked to the window and looked up at the high, familiar skyline of the mountains, daydreaming beyond them to the plains, the hills, and the unknown seas. A pale blue moon, like the stone into which Lori still stared, entranced, floated up quietly over the rim of the clouds around the mountain; and very gently, rain began to fall.

"Some day," he said, offhand, "I suppose someone will give those moons—and this world—a name."

"Some day," Camilla said, "but we'll never know."

A century later they named the planet DARKOVER. But Earth knew nothing of them for two thousand years.